Music in American Life

*Volumes in the series Music in American Life
are listed at the end of this book.*

SECULAR MUSIC IN COLONIAL ANNAPOLIS

SECULAR MUSIC IN COLONIAL ANNAPOLIS

THE TUESDAY CLUB
1745–56

JOHN BARRY TALLEY

UNIVERSITY OF ILLINOIS PRESS
Urbana and Chicago

Publication of this work was supported in part by a grant
from the
Andrew W. Mellon Foundation.

This book is printed on acid-free paper.

Library of Congress Cataloging-in-Publication Data

Talley, John B., 1943–
  Secular music in colonial Annapolis.

  (Music in American life)
  Includes bibliographies and index.
    1. Music—Maryland—Annapolis—18th century—History
and criticism.   2. Tuesday Club (Annapolis, Md.)
3. Annapolis (Md.)—History.   4. Music—Maryland—
Annapolis—18th century.   I. Title.   II. Series.
ML200.8.A552T87   1988   780'.9752'56   86–24992
ISBN 0–252–01402–2 (alk. paper)

for my wife
Marcia Dutton Talley

CONTENTS

Index 307

PREFACE

This study is divided into two sections: Part I is a detailed examination of music in colonial Annapolis, relying on contemporaneous newspapers, letters, journals, estate inventories, and, in particular, the voluminous documents that describe the activities of the Tuesday Club, a social club that flourished in the Maryland capital from 1745 to 1756. Part II is a modern edition of music composed by various members of the Tuesday Club, together with a transcription of the manuscript book of minuets, dated 1758, belonging to the Annapolis dancing master John Ormsby.

Much of the quoted material in this study has been transcribed from the eighteenth-century manuscripts of Alexander Hamilton, an Annapolis physician from 1738 to 1756. Hamilton left two versions of the activities of the Tuesday Club: the minutes of each meeting, which he called "Records" (see the companion volume to this work, edited by Elaine G. Breslaw), and a three-volume, 1,800-page "History." While the records and history agree in their descriptions of meetings or, as Hamilton called them, "sederunts" (literally, "they sat"), I have quoted the accounts in the history, thereby enabling the reader to compare parallel passages in that source and in Breslaw's edition of the records. In footnotes citing both documents, the version actually quoted is the first noted. The music commentaries of the history are, on the whole, more detailed, and, although their use of facetious pseudonyms is at times confusing, the history better reflects the humorous aspect of the organization. In these passages inconsistencies of spelling, punctuation, and capitalization have been preserved. The differences between modern English usage and Hamilton's eighteenth-century style are so numerous that I have not indicated discrepancies by the use of the conventional *sic*, and I must ask the reader to trust that the peculiarities of language in the quoted passages are accurate transcriptions and not typographical errors. While spelling and punctuation are usually clear in these manuscripts, capitalization is often ambiguous. In the case of letters whose form differed between upper- and lowercase, the transcription was easy. But many letters, *C* and *S*, for instance, take the same shape, differing only in size—and that difference is often imperceptible. In fact, all of Hamilton's *S*s appear to be capital letters. In general initial words of sentences were capitalized, but not necessarily initial words of lines in poetry and verse; first letters of proper nouns were capitalized, but many other nouns also begin with uppercase letters, sometimes provided for emphasis, although not with any real consistency or pattern to their application. The use of the apostrophe follows Hamilton's more common practice as in thro', 'till, and 'twas, and appropriate apostrophes have been added for the purpose of consistency where their omission seems to be an obvious form of shorthand. Superscripts have been lowered and periods inserted after all abbreviations.

In editing Hamilton's music manuscript, I have attempted to render the work more performable by offering suggestions enclosed in brackets. These should enable the performer to avoid unlikely dissonances and should provide plausible copy where portions of the manuscript are illegible. However, in the many sections that are tonally ambiguous, performers are encouraged to use their own judgment. While it is sometimes possible to clarify certain harmonic progressions or successions, such "improvements" do not necessarily serve the interests of authenticity and should be questioned. Nevertheless, it is unlikely that blatant dissonances would have been accepted by Hamilton's contemporaries; consequently, a performance that faithfully reproduces sounds that would have been perceived as "wrong" even by rank amateurs of the eighteenth century can hardly be termed "authentic."

The problem of key signatures and accidentals is particularly difficult. Key signatures do not always correspond to the obvious tonal center—G major with two sharps, for instance—and one line of a trio may not bear the same key signature as another line. Nevertheless, the music written by club members was firmly aligned to the major-minor system of tonality. Contradictory key signatures probably represent Hamilton's failure to record correctly the appropriate number of sharps or flats, rather than indicate transposed modal passages. Similarly, the use of accidentals has been made consistent, although here, too, editorial suggestions have been enclosed in brackets.

Where note heads are unclear, the manuscripts often provide clues: stems identify rhythm, and their direction usually determines whether the note was on the upper or lower half of the staff. Where the entire staff is missing, plausible measures have been invented. These reconstructions (indicated by the abbreviation *conj.* [conjecture]) are based on existing portions of the manuscripts and the rules of mid-eighteenth-century counterpoint, which varied only in slight degree from one composer to another. Where two of the three lines are legible, the illegible line can be deduced with a high degree of accuracy. Even with only one clear line, the other two can still be reconstructed through a careful analysis of the music surrounding the missing measures, especially in sequential passages. In this music melodic and rhythmic figurations of individual lines, having been derived from opening motives, generally remain constant throughout a given movement. One can therefore construct passages to fill in missing portions of the manuscript, even to the extent of replacing all three staves for brief sections. While it is not possible to guarantee the absolute accuracy of these passages, it can be stated with some confidence that they are not far off the mark. Furthermore, where the musical form is clear and the harmonic sequence well defined, as they are in the Tuesday Club manuscripts, such reconstruction should be very successful.

Ornamentation has also been suggested. Performers are advised to excercise their judgment in selecting which, and what kind, of ornaments are to be employed, consistent with the practice of the period in the British Isles. For a contemporaneous treatise that includes ornaments, see Francesco Geminiani's *Art of Playing on the Violin* (1740). It would be neither appropriate nor desirable to attempt to execute all suggested ornaments, and performers should use additional ornaments where they see fit, so long as the application is consistent. Specific ornaments have not been suggested, except for mordents, where the melodic line better fits that ornament. Cadential trills are almost always appropriate, and elaboration of extended notes is usually desirable. I might suggest two general rules: always begin trills and turns on the upper auxiliary note (mordents beginning on the principal tone), and terminate longer trills with a final turn or anticipation. The tradition of improvised ornaments was well known to Annapolis musicians in the eighteenth century. Bacon's music manuscripts contain ornaments, and Hamilton's descriptions of performances often mention "gracings and shakings." A performance that did not include appropriate improvised ornamentation could hardly be considered authentic or accurate.

ACKNOWLEDGMENTS

I am deeply indebted to the libraries of The Johns Hopkins University and Maryland Historical Society for permitting me to transcribe the music in their various Tuesday Club documents and for giving me direct access to these rare and fragile materials. I also wish to thank the Library and Museum of the Performing Arts, Lincoln Center, for permission to photograph and transcribe John Ormsby's manuscript book of minuets. I am especially grateful to the music librarians of the Library of Congress for allowing me to examine their extensive collection of eighteenth-century British song sources, and to the librarians of the John Work Garrett Collections, Evergreen House of The Johns Hopkins University Library, for lending their microfilm copy of Hamilton's "History of the Ancient and Honorable Tuesday Club of Annapolis." Without access to this key source, the completion of this book would not have been possible. Oliver Neighbor, superintendent of the British Library's Music Room, was most gracious, assisting in locating tunes that I was unable to find on this side of the Atlantic; Charles Benson, Department of Early Printed Books, Trinity College Library, Dublin, located Bacon's catch, and Malcolm Taylor, librarian at the British Folk Song Library, London, found the club's favorite catch, "The Great Bell of Lincoln."

I wish to thank Kate Van Winkle Keller, coauthor of *The National Tune Index*, the most valuable single reference work for research on secular music in eighteenth-century America, for her encouragement and support.

My thanks also to Dr. Edward Papenfuse, archivist of the state of Maryland, and Phebe Jacobsen, senior archivist, who introduced me to the invaluable resources of the Maryland Hall of Records. Nancy Baker, cultural historian, allowed me to examine her findings concerning Maryland estate inventories and was generous with her time and advice, and Mr. Garner Ranney, of the Maryland Diocesan Archives, was most helpful in assisting me with the Callister Papers. James Heintze, music librarian of American University, has done most impressive research on music in colonial Annapolis and was generous with his time and advice.

This book owes much to J. A. Leo Lemay, whose thorough scholarship provided literary background material as well as biographical information on several of the major figures in this study.

My copyist, Tina Davidson, was a delight. She not only copied my transcriptions of Tuesday Club music but returned again and again to the nearly illegible original manuscripts, attempting to make the performing editions as accurate as possible.

I am especially indebted to Irving Lowens, who was my advisor at the beginning of the dissertation that became this book, and to Dr. Richard Higgins and Dr. Arno Drucker, who also read the dissertation with kindness and encouragement. To my advisor, Dr. Margery Lowens, my deepest appreciation.

Another special acknowledgment goes to an old friend, Dr. Ray Sprenkle of The Johns Hopkins University's Peabody Institute, who suggested this topic and whose own dissertation on Louis Cheslock touched on the Saturday Night Club, an organization whose philosophical roots extend back to the Tuesday Club. His encouragement was a help in time of need.

This book would never have come to press without the assistance and support of Dr. Elaine Breslaw, editor of the *Records of the Tuesday Club of Annapolis, 1745–56* and professor of history at Morgan State University. She conceived the joint project, promoted it with all her considerable ability, and patiently endured my inexperienced efforts in researching and writing about colonial Maryland.

Lastly, to my wife, Marcia, for her personal support and her editorial assistance, my enduring gratitude.

PART I

1

INTRODUCTION

Investigation of secular music in Great Britain's American colonies has been impeded by the scarcity of extant works composed by colonial musicians and a paucity of detailed information concerning musical performances. Contemporaneous accounts of concerts and balls, of music in the theater, the tavern, and the home occasionally identify performers, but colonial repertoire is a matter of considerable speculation. The majority of settlers were from the British Isles; moreover, there is substantial evidence that British popular songs and dances were well known in the colonies.[1] Communication with England was excellent; the adoption of Continental fashions was accomplished in a matter of weeks,[2] and publications from across the Atlantic were reprinted in colonial newspapers within days of their arrival in local post offices. Thomas Wertenbaker, a noted twentieth-century cultural historian, observed that "eighteenth-century American culture was the culture of contemporaneous England transplanted in America and superimposed upon the various civilizations that had developed there."[3]

The individual character of each "civilization" was an important factor in shaping the culture of a particular region. British society in the northern colonies was influenced by New England Puritans and Pennsylvania Quakers, whose religious and moral convictions led them to seek refuge from England in the New World. They wished to be free from her religious and political influence, had little desire to imitate her ways, and even legislated against such frivolous entertainments as the theater.[4] Such was not the case in the southern colonies, where the plantation economy produced a squirearchy that resembled the landed gentry of the mother country.[5] William Black, writing of a visit to Annapolis in 1744, gave the following description of an evening's entertainment:

> We were received by his Excellency and his Lady in the Hall, where we were an hour Entertain'd by them, with some Glasses

of Punch in the intervals of a discourse; then the scene was chang'd to a Dining Room, where you saw a plain proof of the Great Plenty of the Country, a Table in the most Splendent manner set out with Great Variety of Dishes, all serv'd up in the most Elegant way, afterwhich came a dessert no less Curious; Among the Rarities of which it was compos'd was some fine Ice Cream which, with the Strawberries and Milk, eat most Deliciously.[6]

Referring to another occasion, Black noted that "the Governor and some other Gentlemen . . . gave a Ball in the Council Room. . . . "[7] There are many references to horse racing, dancing, card playing, drinking, and elegant dining that testify to the wealthy landowners' imitation of their British counterparts.[8] So it was in Charleston, Williamsburg, and Annapolis that the worldly pleasures of eighteenth-century England were most evident.

Colonial music was, for the most part, composed and performed by musical amateurs. During the period encompassed by this study, America could boast only a few professional musicians such as Charleston's Carl Theodore Pachelbel, Williamsburg's Peter Pelham, Philadelphia's John Palma, and Charles Love, harpsichordist for Hallam's traveling theater company. Most of America's earliest composers were craftsmen or tradesmen, such as William Billings, a tanner by profession, and gentlemen amateurs, such as Francis Hopkinson; but their musical contribution began in the decade following the Tuesday Club years. Hopkinson, a lawyer, writer, statesman, and signer of the Declaration of Independence, is often credited with the composition of the first American song in 1759. James Lyon, a Presbyterian minister, is best known for his collection *Urania* (Philadelphia, [1761]), containing psalm tunes, anthems, and hymns. According to a notice in the *Pennsylvania Gazette*, a Lyon anthem and a Hopkinson ode were performed at a public commencement program given by the College of Pennsylvania on May 23, 1761.[9]

But ten years earlier another ode had been performed in the State House in Annapolis to commemorate the sixth anniversary of the founding of the Tuesday Club. Composed and performed by several club members, its subject matter was too specialized to warrant publication; nevertheless, manuscript copies of three anniversary odes and miscellaneous original instrumental compositions are preserved in "The History of the Ancient and Honorable Tuesday Club," a fanciful account written by Alexander Hamilton between 1754 and 1756, the last years of the club's existence,[10] and in the club records, factual accounts of each meeting from its founding in 1745.[11] This music constitutes the oldest body of secular music composed in America and, with the club's favorite songs and catches, forms the basis of this study.

NOTES

1. Joy Van Cleef and Kate Van Winkle Keller, "Selected American Country Dances and Their English Sources," in *Music in Colonial Massachusetts, 1630–1820*, vol. 1, *Music in Public Places*, Publications of the Colonial Society of Massachusetts, vol. 53 (Boston: Colonial Society of Massachusetts, 1980), pp. 11–12.

2. Louis B. Wright, *The Cultural Life of the American Colonies, 1607–1763* (New York: Harper and Row, 1957), p. 153.

3. Thomas J. Wertenbaker, *The Golden Age of Colonial Culture* (New York: New York University Press, 1942), p. 151.

4. Ibid., pp. 154–55. Richard B. Davis, *Intellectual Life in the Colonial South* (Knoxville: University of Tennessee Press, 1978), 3:1284; the entire chapter "The Fine Arts in the Southern Colonies," pp. 1117–306, comprises an excellent cultural overview.

5. Aubrey C. Land, "The Colonial Period," in *The Old Line State*, ed. Morris L. Radoff (Baltimore: Historical Record Assoc., 1956), p. 22; idem, *Colonial Maryland* (Millwood, N.Y.: Krause-Thomas, 1981), pp. xvi, 124–27, 274–77.

6. William Black, "Journal of William Black," ed. R. A. Brock, *Pennsylvania Magazine of History and Biography* 1 (1877): 126.

7. Ibid., p. 130.

8. Announcements and advertisements in the *Maryland Gazette*, Alexander Hamilton's *Itinerarium*, and Hamilton's "History of the Ancient and Honorable Tuesday Club," for example.

9. Gilbert Chase, *America's Music: From the Pilgrims to the Present*, 2d rev. ed. (New York: McGraw-Hill, 1966), pp. 125–26.

10. Alexander Hamilton, "The History of the Ancient and Honorable Tuesday Club," a three-volume autograph manuscript, is located in the John Work Garrett Collections, Evergreen House of The Johns Hopkins University Library, Baltimore, Md. A small portion of volume 3 (pp. 503–64) is in the Dulany Papers, MS. 1265, Manuscripts Division, Maryland Historical Society, Baltimore. Robert J. Micklus, "Dr. Alexander Hamilton's 'The History of the Tuesday Club,'" 4 vols. (Ph.D. diss., University of Delaware, 1980), is an annotated typescript of Hamilton's history, including facsimile reproductions of the music. Micklus's dissertation is scheduled for publication by the University of North Carolina Press for the Institute of Early American History and Culture, Williamsburg, Va.

11. Alexander Hamilton's annotated minutes of the Tuesday Club constitute the companion volume to this publication; the original manuscripts are divided among three collections: The Johns Hopkins University (hereafter JHU), Maryland Historical Society, and the Library of Congress. "Annapolis, Md. Tuesday Club Record Book," the actual book of minutes recorded in or immediately following the club's meetings, is located in the Garrett Collections, Evergreen House of the JHU Library. "Record of the Tuesday Club, Vol. I," Hamilton's fair copy of the original minutes, covering the first ten years of club meetings (sederunts 1–239), is in the Manuscripts Division (MS. 854), Maryland Historical Society. "Record of the Tuesday Club, Vol. II" covers the final 13 sederunts (240–52) and is housed in the Peter Force Collection, Manuscripts Division, Library of Congress, Washington, D.C. (microfilm mss 17137, reel no. 68, item 170).

2

CONTEXTS OF ORGANIZED MUSIC MAKING IN COLONIAL ANNAPOLIS

History

During its first century Maryland was peopled by Roman Catholics, Quakers, Congregationalists, Puritans, Presbyterians, and other Anglican dissenters, as well as by members of the Church of England; it was administered by a series of Roman Catholic and Protestant governors who were, in turn, ruled by the Puritan Cromwell and by Catholic and Protestant kings and queens of Scottish, Dutch, and Germanic origin.[1] Such diversity required acceptance of the right to a wide variety of political and religious beliefs and produced a fertile climate for the toleration of many public and private amusements suppressed in areas dominated by people of common philosophical and religious persuasions.

By the late seventeenth century, the population center of Maryland had shifted to the north, away from the old capital at St. Mary's City. The Maryland assembly, led by Governor Francis Nicholson, acted in 1694 to relocate the capital of the province in Anne Arundel Town on the Severn River. This new city became known as Annapolis and soon attained a position of prominence in the colonies. John McMahon, one of Maryland's earliest historians, wrote:

> From the period of the grant of its charter by Governor Seymour, Annapolis was continually on the advance. It never acquired a large population, nor any great degree of commercial consequence; but long before the American revolution, it was conspicuous as the seat of wealth and fashion. The luxurious habits, elegant accomplishments, and profuse hospitality of its inhabitants were proverbially known throughout the colonies. It was the seat of a wealthy government, and of its principal institutions; and as such, congregated around it many, whose liberal attainments eminently qualified them for society.[2]

The wealth of the land, literally and figuratively, was tobacco,[3] which was used as currency to purchase goods and to pay taxes. As a crop it encouraged the development of large plantations, consolidated wealth into a few hands, and provided an exportable commodity that made possible the importation of English goods and fashions. More important, its cultivation and preservation included seasons of inactivity during which planters gathered in Annapolis to carry on the business of government and sustained periods of intense social activity, requiring musicians for balls, parties, and other entertainments.

That Annapolis never became as large as the great cities of the northern colonies should not be taken as an indication of its relative importance but rather as an aspect of tidewater commerce. Arthur E. Karinen, writing in 1965, explained that the lack of towns in tidewater Maryland can be attributed to the ready availability of water transportation and to the ability of tobacco ships to load and unload at each plantation, thereby eliminating the need for large port cities.[4] The relative economic and social importance of the large cities to the north can probably be more accurately represented by a comparison of county rather than town populations. According to Karinen, Anne Arundel County surpassed 10,000 inhabitants by 1733;[5] Greene and Harrington's study of early American populations states that the county containing New York City had a population of only 8,622 in 1731.[6] As a colonial capital Annapolis governed a populace about the same size as Virginia, smaller than that of Massachusetts or Pennsylvania, and larger than Connecticut, New York, or the Carolinas.[7]

Annapolis attained its peak of power and influence during the years immediately following the Revolutionary War when, as a meeting place of the Continental Congress, it served as America's capital. Between 1745 and 1756 it was a city already on the rise, capable of attracting and entertaining some of the liveliest intellects of the day.[8]

The Exchange of Ideas

Opportunity for the exchange and dissemination of ideas among all learned citizens was provided by the state printer, William Parks, who founded the *Maryland Gazette* in 1727 and was, from 1726 until 1737, publisher for the Maryland legislature.[9] He printed pamphlets, original essays, articles, letters, poems, sermons, announcements, and advertisements from local citizens, merchants, and craftsmen, as well as foreign and domestic news, often reprinting private letters and published articles from other periodicals. Brief items appeared in the *Maryland Gazette;* longer pieces were published separately and usually sold at the printer's shop, which also served as the town post office.

When J. A. Leo Lemay wrote in 1972 that "the existence of a population large enough and with enough interest in literature to pay for the printing of a 68-page quarto Latin and English poem marks a significant step in the development of Maryland literature," he was speaking of Parks's publication in 1728 of Edward Holdsworth's poem *Muscipula*, a satire of the Welsh people that Richard Lewis, the Annapolis schoolmaster who translated it, had entitled *The Mouse-Trap; or, The Battle of the Cambrians and Mice.*[10] Ebenezer Cooke's celebrated satire *The Sot-Weed Factor*, which was written in the mock-heroic style of Samuel Butler's *Hudibras*[11] and supposedly described the conditions, manners, customs, and people of Maryland, was composed in 1708. But the third edition, published by Parks in 1731, appeared in the *Maryland Muse*, along with *The History of Col. Nathaniel Bacon's Rebellion in Virginia, Done into Hudibrastick Verse.*[12] Notable characteristics of Maryland's humorous poetry were aptly described by translator Richard Lewis in his preface to Holdsworth's *Muscipula:* "This poem, is of the *Mock heroic*, or *Burlesque* Kind, of which there are *two* sorts. One, describes a *ludicrous Action*, in *Heroic Verse*; such is *The Rape of the Lock*. The *Other* under *low Characters*, and in *odd, uncommon* Numbers, debases some great Event; as *Butler* has done, in his celebrated *Hudibras*; which would have been still more *truly comical* in the opinion of an *excellent Judge*, if it had been written in the *Heroic Measure*."[13] As we shall see, this mock-heroic, satirical style was a hallmark of the Tuesday Club poetry, and four of the club's founding members subscribed to *Muscipula.*[14]

Parks's successor was the remarkable Jonas Green, poet laureate of the Tuesday Club, who served Maryland as state printer from 1738 until his death in 1767. The *Maryland Gazette*, which had ceased publication in 1734,[15] was revived in 1745 by Green, who continued the encouragement of native literature by soliciting and printing local literary endeavors. Among his contributors were two prominent Tuesday Club members, Dr. Alexander Hamilton and the Reverend Thomas Bacon. Both Green and Parks published a wide range of material, but Green printed more of it in his expanded *Gazette*.

In addition to publicly and privately publishing the poems, essays, letters, and sermons of local writers, Green printed the acts of the Maryland legislature and kept the readers of his *Gazette* well informed with the latest news from foreign and domestic cities. His descriptions of local events have shed much light on the social and cultural activity of the Maryland capital. A sample of his reporting follows:

> On Wednesday the 27th ult. being the festival of St. John the Evangelist, and the Anniversary of the Ancient and Honorable Fraternity of Free and Accepted Masons, the Gentlemen of the Brotherhood, belonging to the Lodge in this City . . . celebrated

the Day in the following Manner: At Twelve o'Clock they went in Procession, with white Gloves and Aprons, from the House of their Brother Middleton, being preceded by their Master, Wardens, and Grand Stewards, to the Church, where an excellent Sermon, adapted to the Occasion, was preached by their Brother, the Rev. Mr. Brogden: After Sermon, they returned in the same Manner from Church to the Indian King, where, having dined elegantly, they elected their Master and Officers for the ensuing Year; and then proceeded in the above Order to the great Council Room, where they made a ball for the Entertainment of the Ladies, and the Evening was spent with innocent Mirth and Gayety.[16]

The *Gazette* of this period was sprinkled with paradoxes, riddles, occasional bits of bawdiness, and other literary amusements, some of which were undoubtedly composed by Green himself. Even poetry from the Tuesday Club as well as occasional mention of its members' antics appeared in the colonial newspaper.

It is, however, the advertisements and announcements of the *Gazette* that provide the most valuable information about mid-century Annapolis. The increase of commercial activity is vividly displayed by the scope and diversity of these notices. Announcements of imported goods sold in both stores and homes were a weekly occurrence. Advertisements of tanners, saddlers, wigmakers, whipmakers, dancing instructors, tutors of all subjects, chair- and cabinetmakers, gold- and silversmiths, tavern keepers, shoemakers, staymakers, carpenters, and even a musician for balls and other entertainments fill the *Gazette*'s back pages. Rewards were offered for the return of lost and stolen goods, and notices advised the citizenry of concerts, plays, and ballad operas.

Mid-century Annapolis could also boast writers of major importance; its greatest literary figures were James Sterling, Thomas Bacon, and Alexander Hamilton, whose cultural contributions will be considered in the following chapters. It is noteworthy that all three men were involved with the Tuesday Club.

Theater

Evidence suggests that plays, farces, dramas, and ballad operas were well known in Annapolis in the first half of the eighteenth century. A *Maryland Gazette* theatrical notice of May 26, 1730, is one of America's earliest, and Jonas Green advertised "History of Theatres," "A Volume of Plays," and "Single Plays" in his *Gazette* of December 4, 1751. Collections of plays also appear in Maryland's eighteenth-century estate inventories, and Alexander Hamilton included a proposal for improving the theater, both structurally and dramatically, in his history of the Tuesday Club.[17] The

many Marylanders who had emigrated from the British Isles were surely
familiar with the English theatrical tradition; of particular interest is the
Reverend James Sterling, rector of All Hallows Parish, Anne Arundel
County, from 1737 to 1739, and of St. Anne's Parish, Annapolis, from
1739 to 1740. This theatrical clergyman was also the author of the first
tragedy known to have been written by a native of Ireland, *The Rival Gen-
erals* (Dublin, 1722), and was the widower of a professional actress noted
for her portrayal of Polly Peachum in John Gay's *Beggar's Opera*. In 1740
Sterling settled in Chestertown, Maryland, as rector of St. Paul's church.[18]
Although only an occasional guest at the Tuesday Club, he remained a
close friend of several members and was assisted in his other position as
"Collector of His Majesty's Duties" by William Lux, a prominent Tuesday
Club musician.[19] His involvement with theater continued in America. For
the appearance of Hallam's company in Chestertown in January 1760,
Sterling composed a prologue, which was repeated at the company's An-
napolis opening in March of the same year.[20]

Despite an apparently receptive audience, theatrical productions
were an occasional event; in the Tuesday Club era most occurred during a
single extended season, June to December 1752. Although no other performances have been documented during the Tuesday Club years, various unidentified "strolling players" probably entertained occasionally in
Annapolis.[21] One group, headed by Thomas Kean and Walter Murray,
performed in New York and Philadelphia in 1749 and appeared in several Maryland and Virginia cities in the 1751–52 season. This was the
"Company of Comedians from Virginia" who staged no less than seven-
teen productions in Annapolis in 1752.[22] Instead of leaving Annapolis,
they used the town as a base of operations, returning to it after performances in Upper Marlborough and Chestertown. Their theater productions are chronicled in the *Maryland Gazette* (see table 1).

The theatrical events itemized in table 1 reveal much about the music
of the period and the public contributions of Tuesday Club musicians.
Two of the productions were advertised as operas: *The Beggar's Opera*,
first and foremost of its genre, and *Damon and Philida*. Additionally,
several of the "farces" performed as afterpieces were also ballad operas. Among these were *The Devil to Pay*, *The Virgin Unmask'd*, and *The
Beau in the Suds*.[23] Such abbreviated afterpieces were a regular feature
of eighteenth-century theater. As Edmond M. Gagey wrote in his 1937
study of ballad opera: "Since the beginning of the century, however,
the afterpiece had become virtually a necessary appendix to all stage
productions. It was here that, along with the non-musical farces, ballad
opera found a real mission and *raison d'être*. Not only were short pieces
constantly being written and produced to satisfy the demand, but many
of the longer operas . . . were promptly reduced to one or two acts."[24]
Coffey's *Devil to Pay*, for example, one of the most successful ballad operas

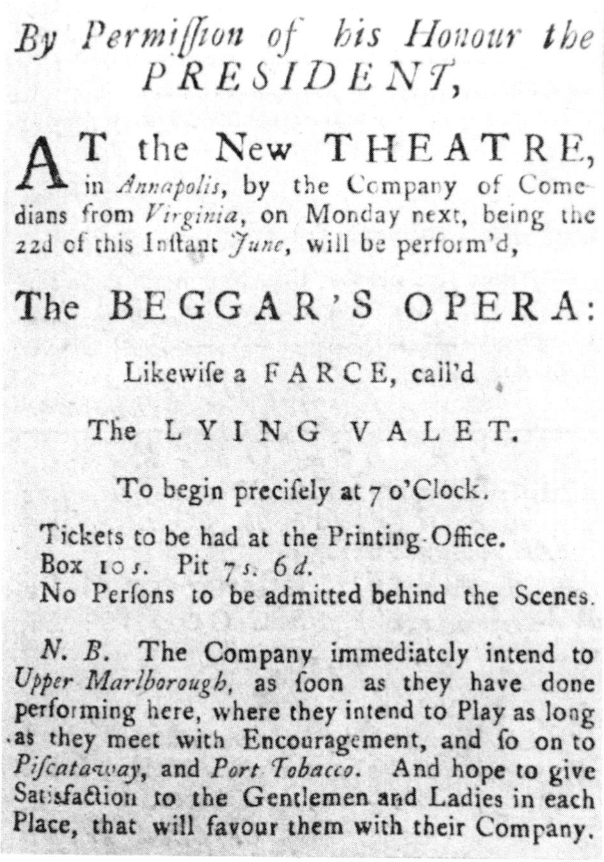

By Permiſſion of his Honour the
PRESIDENT,

AT the New THEATRE,
in *Annapolis*, by the Company of Comedians from *Virginia*, on Monday next, being the
22d of this Inſtant *June*, will be perform'd,

The BEGGAR'S OPERA:

Likewiſe a FARCE, call'd

The LYING VALET.

To begin preciſely at 7 o'Clock.

Tickets to be had at the Printing-Office.
Box 10 s. Pit 7 s. 6 d.
No Perſons to be admitted behind the Scenes.

N. B. The Company immediately intend to
Upper Marlborough, as ſoon as they have done
performing here, where they intend to Play as long
as they meet with Encouragement, and ſo on to
Piſcataway, and *Port Tobacco*. And hope to give
Satisfaction to the Gentlemen and Ladies in each
Place, that will favour them with their Company.

Figure 1. *Maryland Gazette*, June 18, 1752

of the century, was reduced from a full-length work to an afterpiece
by Theophilis Cibber immediately following its premier performance
in 1731.[25]

Annapolis experienced at least twelve nights of theater in 1752; six
of those evenings included ballad opera, and many of the plays also
featured singing and dancing. Although probably supported by a harpsichord, these musical productions could easily have been performed
without instrumental accompaniment. Songs from such stage works constitute the largest body of popular music performed in Annapolis that
can be identified with reasonable accuracy (see appendix A).[26]

A *Maryland Gazette* advertisement for *The Beggar's Opera* (fig. 2) in
September 1752 is of particular importance to this study. It is the earliest
announcement of an American performance of opera with orchestral accompaniment that has come to light; furthermore, the advertisement illustrates the interrelationship among Masons, music, gentlemen, and, as

TABLE 1

Theater in Annapolis, 1752

Date	Production
June 22	*The Beggar's Opera* (ballad opera) *The Lying Valet*
July 6	*The Busy Body* *The Lying Valet*
July 13	*The Beau Stratagem* *The Virgin Unmask'd* (ballad opera)
July 20	*The Recruiting Officer* *The Beau in the Suds; or, The Female Parson* (ballad opera)
July 27	*The London Merchant; or, The History of George Barnwell* *Damon and Philida; or, Love in a Riddle* (ballad opera)
July 31	*A Bold Stroke for a Wife* *The Beau in the Suds* (ballad opera)
Aug. 3	*The Drummer; or, The Haunted House* *The Devil to Pay; or, The Wives Metamorphos'd* (ballad opera)
Aug. 20[a]	*The Beggar's Opera* (ballad opera) *The Lying Valet*
Sept. 14[a]	*The Beggar's Opera* (ballad opera) *The Lying Valet*
Oct. 2	*The Constant Couple; or, A Trip to the Jubilee* *The Lying Valet*
Oct. 26[b]	*The Beggar's Opera* (ballad opera) *The Lying Valet*
Dec. 11	*Richard III* *Miss in Her Teens*
Dec. 13	*The Constant Couple* *The Anatomist; or, Sham Doctor*
Dec. 16[c]	*Richard III* *The Lying Valet*

Source: issues of the *Maryland Gazette*, June–Dec. 1752.

[a] produced in Upper Marlborough
[b] produced in Chestertown
[c] benefit performance for Bacon's charity school

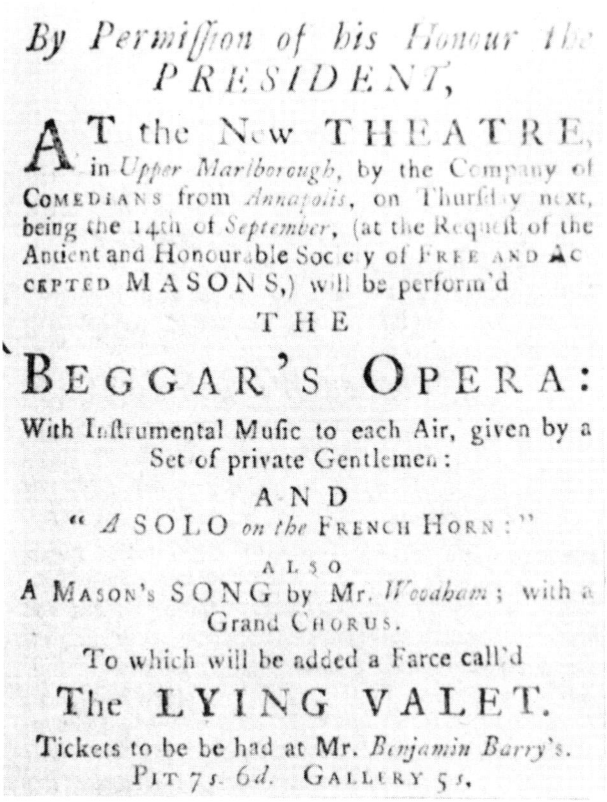

By Permiſſion of his *Honour the*
PRESIDENT,

AT the New THEATRE, in *Upper Marlborough*, by the Company of COMEDIANS from *Annapolis*, on Thurſday next, being the 14th of *September*, (at the Requeſt of the Antient and Honourable Society of FREE AND AC CEPTED MASONS,) will be perform'd

THE

BEGGAR'S OPERA:

With Inſtrumental Muſic to each Air, given by a Set of private Gentlemen:

AND

" *A* SOLO *on the* FRENCH HORN:"

ALSO

A MASON's SONG by Mr. *Wooaham*; with a Grand CHORUS.

To which will be added a Farce call'd

The LYING VALET.

Tickets to be be had at Mr. *Benjamin Barry's.*
PIT 7*s.* 6*d.* GALLERY 5*s.*

Figure 2. *Maryland Gazette*, September 7, 1752

James Heintze first noted in 1978, the Tuesday Club as well. Several members of the club participated in the Annapolis Masonic society, including Hamilton, who was its first grand master, and Jonas Green, its secretary.[27] The term *gentlemen* in the eighteenth century was applied exclusively to members of the upper social classes. Many, if not most, musical "gentlemen" of Annapolis were associated with the Tuesday Club. Additionally, Jonas Green was the only known horn player in the area. A study of instrumental music composed by and for Tuesday Club members reveals that the number of performers and their probable level of skill was more than adequate for a satisfactory rendering of the Pepusch orchestration. The club, in 1752, could muster at least five string players, two flutists, a keyboard performer, and possibly a bassoonist. Clearly possessing musical means, Masonic motive, and opportunity, the "private Gentlemen" cited in the notice must have been none other than the Tuesday Club musicians.

Little else is known about this theatrical season. No descriptions of its productions have been discovered, but a *Maryland Gazette* advertisement of July 2, 1752, suggests that the company had costumes and scenery: "No Persons to be admitted behind the Scenes," and "As the Company have now got their Hands, Cloaths, &c. compleat. . . ." The *Gazette*'s theater notice of December 7, 1752, contains the only published description of the Annapolis theater: "N.B. The House is entirely lined throughout, fit for the Reception of Ladies and Gentlemen; and they have also raised a Porch at the Door, that will keep out the Inclemency of the Weather." Tickets for the productions cost ten shillings for a box, seven shillings and sixpence for a place in the pit, and five shillings for a seat in the gallery,[28] possibly indicating a fair-sized hall, whose location, however, is unknown. Most Annapolis historians do not believe that a theater in the modern sense existed at all, but that the plays and operas were produced in warehouses, as was often the case in this period.[29]

Recreations

Public recreations included spring and fall fairs, which invariably centered on horse racing. Baltimore hosted a fair on October 10 through 12, 1745, and Anne Arundel County on October 30 through 31 of the same year.[30] Activities included awarding prizes for the best-woven linen and the best steer, "cudgeling" (fighting with clubs), wrestling, and foot races.[31] Although Annapolis might host only one such event each season, there was ample opportunity to attend similar festivities in neighboring towns and counties. The *Maryland Gazette* carried many notices for fairs and horse races in "Baltimore Town," Prince George's County, Upper Marlborough, and as far away as Frederick, Maryland, and Leeds, Virginia.[32] In addition to racing, Annapolitans enjoyed other traditional forms of gaming: dice and cards, billiards and backgammon, shuffleboard, nine pins, and a single team sport, cricket.[33]

Fairs and horse races were often followed by balls for the gentry;[34] balls seem to have been the favorite form of upper-class social activity and were held in celebration of practically anything: the birthdays of Lord Baltimore and the Prince of Wales, victories of the English over the French, and St. George's day were all accompanied by balls and other less elegant festivities for the general populace.[35] The local *Gazette* of April 29, 1746, described a typical public celebration as follows: "Wednesday being the Festival of St. George, the same was observed here by a Number of Gentlemen of English Birth, Descent, and Principle, in an elegant manner. The same day the Exit of the Rebellion was celebrated by firing of Guns, drinking loyal Healths, and other Demonstrations of Joy. There was a Ball in the Evening, the whole City was illuminated, and a great

Quantity of Punch given amongst the Populace at the Bonfire, on this Occasion."

Balls were hosted by high government officials and also by private citizens and organizations. Governor Horatio Sharpe was a frequent host; one of his parties was described in the *Gazette* of September 13, 1753: "Thursday Evening last, his Excellency the Governor gave a Ball in the Council Room, where was a numerous and charming Appearance of Ladies and a great Concourse of Gentlemen. His Excellency tarry'd 'till the breaking up of the Ball, at Twelve o'Clock." This "Council Room," the council chamber of the Maryland State House, was probably the largest public room in the city and certainly the favorite site for aristocratic celebrations. A ball held there in February 1754, to honor Lord Baltimore's twenty-third birthday, continued until 2:00 A.M.[36] The Annapolis Freemason's Society sponsored a ball on December 27, 1749, to mark their anniversary (cited earlier in this chapter) as did the Tuesday Club on December 31, 1745. Both dances were held in the council chamber. Hamilton wrote a detailed description of the latter:

> The ball then was held at the time appointed, which happened to be an extreme cold night, and therefore the better for dancing. There were a great many Ladies and Gentlemen, and most of the members of the Club attended, the cake was froze, but the wine and punch retained their liquidity, the longstanding members that chose to dance, danced, and those that chose not, looked on; and drank a bumper now and then to expand the animal spirits, by the frigid air drove to the centre. There were danced many minuets, country dances & jiggs, and there was much bowing, cringing, complimenting, curtsying, oggling, flurting, and smart repartees, as is usual on such occasions, and the Reverend Mr. Sly [John Gordon], tho' the gravity of his cloth, would not permit him to dance, yet he made by much the smartest figure, in squiring the Ladies comparing them, as they stood in a row, to the milky way. . . . In fine, everything was conducted with great elegance, and mirth prevailed in the company, nothing being wanting to compleat all.[37]

Documents of the Tuesday Club also chronicle less formal dancing. The evening of May 15, 1750, for example, proved hazardous for the rector of St. Anne's church:

> Then several martial tunes were plaid solo, Sir John, Knight and Champion of the Club [John Bullen], dancing several heroic and warlike dances, and honored the Chancellor [Rev. Alexander Malcolm] so far as to dance a Jigg with him, while the latter laid aside the gravity of his office and play'd and danced at one and

the same time, but Sir John, making a faux pas, he fell upon the Chancellor, and almost overset him, and broke the bridge of his fiddle.[38]

In addition to the balls and "elegant entertainments," George Downey held "two penny hops," opportunities for young bachelors and ladies to practice their steps, for which privilege they paid twopence. Hamilton made an oblique reference to this practice in the course of recounting another of the interminable club disputes:

> Mr. Quaint [Edward Dorsey] had wrote a satyr on him [William Thornton] and some others which he entitled the Reverend Scout, in which was a relation of an adventure of Solo Never-out, Esqr. [Thornton], Mr. Secretary Scribble [Hamilton], and Mr. Slyboots Pleasant [Walter Dulany], who had one night a set meeting with some celebrated nymphs of the town, at one of these polite assemblies, called two penny hops, which was held at the house of Mr. George Downie, Musicioner.[39]

No other record of Downey's hops or of his musicianship has been discovered; his profession has been confirmed by the inventory of his estate, which identifies him as "Mr. George Downey, musician."[40]

Instruction in dance was part of the standard educational fare. Charles Peale, schoolmaster at the Kent County School, offered lessons in dancing, and several colonials advertised instruction in their homes. One such notice appeared in the *Maryland Gazette* of November 6, 1755: "John and Mary Rivers, Living in Annapolis, near the Church, Teach Dancing, French, Singing, all Sorts of Embroidery, and every curious Work which can be perform'd with a Needle, suitable for young Ladies." The following week Martha Rogers announced her intention to open a school to teach children dancing.[41] John Ormsby, the dancing master whose advertisements first appeared in 1757, after the demise of the Tuesday Club, offered dancing instruction in Baltimore and Upper Marlborough, as well as Annapolis (see p. 26).[42]

Social Clubs

The Ancient and Honorable Fraternity of Free and Accepted Masons, the first Masonic lodge established in Maryland, was active in Annapolis from 1749.[43] The involvement in this organization of prominent members of the Tuesday Club (noted in the preceding section) underscores the diversity of their contribution to Maryland culture. In addition to Hamilton and Green (master and secretary, respectively), Alexander Malcolm was senior warden and Edward Dorsey, junior warden.[44] John Lomas also served as warden, and the Reverends John Gordon and Thomas Bacon delivered two of the three sermons known to have been preached for the lodge at Annapolis.[45] Although no Masonic records exist that list the membership or describe the activities of the Annapolis lodge,[46] two notices in the *Maryland Gazette* announce the lodge's support and sponsorship of balls and musical theater, underscoring Hamilton's desire to encourage "polite literature and arts" in his capacity as grand master.[47]

The social clubs of the eighteenth century provided welcome opportunities for educated, intelligent people to meet regularly and discuss the concerns of the day. More important to the purposes of this study, their recreational music making constituted one of America's earliest concert idioms. Leo Lemay wrote in 1972 that, "in the golden age of colonial culture, the club was a dominant social institution. Nearly every colonial tavern was the home of at least one club, whose members . . . gathered together to drink, talk, and play music."[48]

The Western Branch Club was active in Prince George's County as early as 1730, but the oldest social club in Maryland is the South River Club, whose records date from the 1720s, earlier documents having been destroyed in a clubhouse fire.[49] The South River Club evidently flourished during the Tuesday Club era; unfortunately its records do not include descriptions of meetings, although its public celebrations were occasionally recorded in the *Maryland Gazette*. In the summer of 1746 the following notice appeared: "The Gentlemen belonging to the ancient South-River Club, to express their Loyalty to his Majesty, on the Success of the inimitable Duke of Cumberland's obtaining a compleat Victory over the Pretender, and delivering us from Persecution at home and Popery and Invasion from abroad, have appointed a grand entertainment to be given at their Club-House on Thursday next. An example worthy the imitation of all true loyal Subjects."[50]

A letter from Chestertown, published in the *Maryland Gazette* of March 24, 1747, affirmed the renown of Maryland's oldest club. The writer referred to clubs on the Western Shore of the Chesapeake—which he believed to exist "in almost every County, well regulated, and sorted like Birds of a Feather (especially that ancient one of South River)"—and requested the editor to "procure me a Copy of some of their Best Rules" to assist him in regulating his own Eastern Shore club. The following year the *Gazette* commended a Loyal Club in Upper Marlborough, but for information about clubs in the Annapolis area, we must return again to Hamilton.[51] In tracing the lineage of the Tuesday Club, his history describes some earlier Annapolitan organizations. Notable among these forerunners were the Red House Club and the Ugly Club, some of whose members joined with Hamilton to found the Tuesday Club after the earlier groups disbanded.[52]

Hamilton deplored the activities of some contemporary clubs, calling them "bouzing or toaping clubs" and claiming, furthermore, that even the local women's organizations were devoted to the pleasures of drinking.[53] In establishing the Tuesday Club, Hamilton sought to remedy certain deficiencies he had observed in other colonial organizations. His low opinion of societies whose primary activity was the consumption of alcohol is clearly expressed in his *Itinerarium*. Of the Hungarian Club of New York he wrote:

> After supper they set in for drinking, to which I was adverse, and therefore sat upon nettles. They filled up bumpers at each round, but I would drink only three, which were to the King, Governour Clinton, and Governour Bladen, which last was my own. Two or three toapers in the company seemed to be of opinion that a man could not have a more sociable quality or enduement than to be able to pour down seas of liquor, and remain unconquered, while others sank under the table. I heard this philosophical maxim, but silently dissented to it. I left the company at ten at night pretty well flushed with my three bumpers, and ruminating on my folly went to my lodging at Mrs. Hogg's in Broad Street.[54]

The writer's aversion is further reflected in a Tuesday Club rule that forbade the opening of any fresh bottle of spirits after 11:00 P.M.[55]

Banality, as perceived by Hamilton, was anathema. He wrote disparagingly of the Philosophical Club of Newport, Rhode Island:

> The company fell upon the disputes and controversies of the fanatics of these parts, their declarations, recantations, letters, advices, remonstrances, and other such damned stuff, of so little consequence to the benefit of mankind or the publick that I looked upon all time spent in either talking concerning them or reading their works as eternally lost and thrown away, and therefore disgusted with such a stupid subject of discourse, I left this Club and went home.[56]

He found the conversation more entertaining at the Governour's Club in Philadelphia, where there was a discussion about English poets and Cervantes, but also noted that "some persons there showed a particular fondness for introducing gross, smutty expressions, which I thought did not altogether become a company of philosophers and men of sense."[57] The Tuesday Club sought to insure a lofty intellectual atmosphere by requiring members to discourse on love, honesty, and other philosophical topics.

Both the records and history of the Tuesday Club contain frequent references to the consumption of quantities of punch, and the documents are certainly not devoid of off-color material; but the drinking of punch was never a primary purpose of the meetings, and there is no evidence of vulgarity for its own sake. Bawdiness typified the period and was integral to the considerable wit and humor of the club.

An important distinction can be made between the Tuesday Club and most other colonial societies: its membership indulged not only in the activities it enjoyed but in those undertakings it thought it should enjoy, thereby achieving a cultural responsibility rarely encountered in similar organizations of the era.

Music

The music of mid-century Annapolis was more recreation than art. Although a few of Maryland's best musicians were acquainted with the works of leading European composers, it was the popular songs and dances of the British Isles that were heard most often in the colonial capital.

Sacred music did not flourish here during this period. Annapolis did not receive the musical benefit of Germans and Moravians who had settled in Pennsylvania and in western Maryland. American Anglican church music was in a period of transition as the old Bay Psalm Book faded in popularity and new collections of psalms and singing methods appeared, such as John Tufts's *Introduction to the Singing of Psalm-Tunes* (Boston?, 1721) and Thomas Walter's *Grounds and Rules of Musick Explained* (Boston, 1721). Many American congregations adopted Nahum Tate's and Nicholas Brady's *New Version of the Psalms of David* (London, 1696), a collection eventually replaced by Isaac Watts's *Psalms of David Imitated* (London, 1719). Watts's religious poetry also became popular following the printing of his *Hymns and Spiritual Songs* (London, 1707).[58] Marylanders were certainly aware of new psalm collections. Henry Callister, in 1747, ordered the "New Sett of Psalm tunes & Anthems, W. S. Sanby," and "Heaven open to all men, J. Robinson."[59] Psalms in Annapolis may have been performed using the old method of lining out the verses, wherein a leader sings one line of a psalm, then the congregation repeats the same line. More likely, St. Anne's very musical rector, Alexander Malcolm, introduced the reforms begun in New England, the location of his former parish. Those reforms sought to train congregations to read music, thereby eliminating the need for lining out and permitting the incorporation of more sophisticated settings of hymns and psalms.[60] This singing was unaccompanied, at least in the most prominent and influential church in the city; Malcolm's musicianship notwithstanding, St. Anne's did not acquire an organ until the 1760s.[61] Secular music, on the other hand, thrived; it was played, sung, danced, and composed by the citizens of the province. Their music, especially that of the Tuesday Club, will be considered in detail in the following chapters.

1. Aubrey C. Land, *Colonial Maryland* (Millwood, N.Y.: Krause-Thomas, 1981), presents a particularly clear description of the relationship between religion and politics in early Maryland.

2. John V. L. McMahon, *Historical View of the Government of Maryland* (Baltimore: Lukas and Deaver, 1831), p. 257.

3. Land, *Colonial Maryland*, pp. 73–74.

4. Arthur E. Karinen, "Numerical and Distributional Aspects of Maryland Population, 1631–1840," *Maryland Historical Magazine* 60 (1965): 141.

5. Arthur E. Karinen, "Maryland Population," *Maryland Historical Magazine* 54 (1959): 377.

6. Evarts B. Greene and Virginia D. Harrington, *American Population before the Federal Census of 1790* (1932; rpt., Gloucester, Mass.: Smith, 1966), p. 97.

7. Ibid., pp. 4–6.

8. See Elaine G. Breslaw's analysis of the city and its population in her introduction to *Records of the Tuesday Club of Annapolis, 1745–56* (Urbana: University of Illinois Press, 1988).

9. Lawrence C. Wroth, *A History of Printing in Colonial Maryland* (Baltimore: Typothetae, 1922), p. 69.

10. J. A. Leo Lemay, *Men of Letters in Colonial Maryland* (Knoxville: University of Tennessee Press, 1972), p. 75.

11. Ibid., p. 77.

12. Wroth, *History of Printing in Colonial Maryland*, p. 179.

13. Edward Holdsworth, *Muscipula: The Mouse-Trap; or, The Battle of the Cambrians & Mice, a Poem . . . Translated into English, by R. Lewis* (Annapolis, Md.: Parks, 1728), p. x.

14. Ibid., pp. xiv–xvi. The four Tuesday Club subscribers were William Cumming, Robert Gordon, John Lomas, and William Rogers.

15. Wroth, *History of Printing in Colonial Maryland*, p. 184.

16. *Maryland Gazette*, Jan. 3, 1750.

17. Alexander Hamilton, "A modest proposal, for the new modelling and Improvement of our Modern Theatre," in Alexander Hamilton, "The History of the Ancient and Honorable Tuesday Club," 3 vols., The Johns Hopkins University Library and Maryland Historical Society, Baltimore, 2 : 181–202.

18. Lemay, *Men of Letters*, pp. 257–62.

19. Donnell M. Owings, *His Lordship's Patronage* (Baltimore: Furst, 1953), p. 182, lists Sterling as "Collector" at Patapsco; the *Maryland Gazette* on Aug. 27, 1752, contains an advertisement by William Lux as "Deputy to Collector of His Majesty's Duties at Patapsco."

20. *Maryland Gazette*, Mar. 6, 1760. Lemay, *Men of Letters*, p. 306, claims Sterling was the author.

21. Louis B. Wright, *The Cultural Life of the American Colonies, 1607–1763* (New York: Harper and Row, 1957), p. 181.

22. Hugh F. Rankin, *The Theater in Colonial America* (Chapel Hill: University of North Carolina Press, 1965), p. 40. This company has often been confused with the more famous troupe headed by Louis Hallam that also performed in Virginia in 1752. Two actors from Hallam's company, Mr. Wynell and Mr. Herbert, appeared in *Richard III* at Annapolis on Dec. 11, 1752; their performance and an earlier advertisement identifying the players as "the Company of Comedians from Virginia" (see fig. 1) are the source of the confusion. Rankin noted that the two performers, inferior actors in Hallam's company, did not perform with Hallam after their Annapolis appearance. The designation "Comedians from Virginia" simply identified their most recent performing location. When the

Kean-Murray company ventured to Upper Marlborough, it was advertised as the "Company of Comedians from Annapolis" (*Maryland Gazette*, Aug. 13, 1752).

23. Edward Ravenscroft's *Sham Doctor*, also known as *The Anatomist*, is not to be confused with Henry Fielding's ballad opera *The Mock Doctor*. George O. Seilhamer, in his *History of the American Theatre* (Philadelphia: Globe Printing House, 1888), p. 33, incorrectly includes both "Doctors" in the Annapolis repertoire; the *Maryland Gazette* lists only Ravenscroft's title and pairs *Beau in the Suds* with *The Recruiting Officer* in its July 16, 1752, edition.

24. Edmond M. Gagey, *Ballad Opera* (New York: Columbia University Press, 1937), pp. 100–101.

25. Roger Fiske, *English Theatre Music in the Eighteenth Century* (London: Oxford University Press, 1973), p. 112.

26. Five different ballad operas and twelve plays were produced on those twelve evenings (see table 1).

27. James R. Heintze, "Alexander Malcolm, Musician, Clergyman, and Schoolmaster," *Maryland Historical Magazine* 73 (1978): 231, includes a possible list of instrumentalists.

28. *Maryland Gazette*, July 23, 1752.

29. For additional information about performers and plays, see Kathryn P. Ward, "The First Professional Theater in Maryland in Its Colonial Setting," *Maryland Historical Magazine* 70 (1975): 29–44.

30. *Maryland Gazette*, Sept. 21, 1745; Oct. 25, 1745.

31. Ibid., Sept. 15, 1747.

32. Ibid., Sept. 27, 1745; May 12, 1747; Apr. 4, 1750; Apr. 26, 1749; July 12, 1749, to name a few.

33. Ibid., Nov. 14, 1754, carried an announcement of the game played by "Eleven South River Gentlemen" who were opposed by a team from Prince George's County; South River was victorious. The *Maryland Gazette* of Jan. 13, 1748, advertised a billiard table, a shuffleboard table, "a good Nine Pin Alley, with good Nine-Pins and Bowls"; and Hamilton, "History" 1:viii, wrote: "How many plod and plod on from day to day, and do nothing but build castles in the air, how many are entertained with a toothpick, a shuttlecock and battledoor, a pair of dice, a cup and ball, a pair of cudgels and foiles, a Race house a fiddle a bagpipe, a french horn a ring of bells and a pack of cards." George Downey's estate inventory, listed in Anne Arundel County Inventories, 1751, Liber 48, fol. 148, included a "backgammon table."

34. *Maryland Gazette*, Sept. 30, 1747, and Oct. 4, 1749, are typical.

35. Ibid., Jan. 3, 1750; Oct. 31, 1750; Feb. 22, 1753; Sept. 13, 1753; Feb. 21, 1754; Sept. 12, 1754; June 5, 1755, indicate that some of these events were celebrated annually.

36. Ibid., Feb. 21, 1754.

37. Hamilton, "History" 1:227–28. See also Breslaw, ed., *Records*, sederunt 26, Dec. 10, 1745.

38. Hamilton, "History" 2:145. See also Breslaw, ed., *Records*, sederunt 130, May 15, 1750.

39. Hamilton, "History" 1:248. The exact date of this event is not known; it was recorded in the history for Mar. 1746.

40. Anne Arundel County Inventories, 1751, Liber 48, fol. 148.

41. *Maryland Gazette*, Nov. 13, 1755.

42. Ibid., Oct. 20, 1757. The number of dancing masters advertising in the *Maryland Gazette* increased in the years immediately following the Tuesday Club era. See James R. Heintze, "Music in Colonial Annapolis" (M.A. thesis, American University, 1969).

43. Edward T. Schultz, *History of Freemasonry in Maryland* (Baltimore: Medairy, 1884), 1:23.

44. Ibid. 3 : 262.

45. Wroth, *History of Printing in Colonial Maryland*, pp. 198–202.

46. According to Schultz, *History of Freemasonry in Maryland* 1 : 23, the Annapolis Lodge was chartered by Thomas Oxnard, provincial grand master of the St. John's Grand Lodge of Massachusetts, and provincial grand master of North America. The application for a constitution is dated "Fryday, July 13th 1750," and was made by "Bro. McDaniel, D.G.M." The constitution was granted on Aug. 12, 5750 [1750]. No other Masonic records concerning this early lodge have come to light. Three sermons, delivered to the lodge and published separately by Jonas Green in 1750 and 1753, include the names of several officers in the dedications. Wroth, *History of Printing in Colonial Maryland*, p. 198, cites the entire dedication of William Brogden's sermon "Freedom and Love" (1750); Lemay, *Men of Letters*, p. 239, quotes a portion of the dedication for John Gordon's Masonic sermon "Brotherly Love Explained and Enforc'd" (1750). The only extant copy of Bacon's sermon (1753) is located in Masonic Hall, Grand Lodge of Massachusetts, Boston. Public announcements of Annapolis Masonic activity ended with Green's death in 1767. A second lodge was chartered in the 1790s, flourished for a few years, and was disbanded. The present lodge dates from 1848.

47. *Maryland Gazette*, Jan. 3, 1750; and Sept. 7, 1752; the quotation is from Hamilton's "Discourse Delivered from the Chair in the Lodge-Room at Annapolis," which was printed with John Gordon's sermon "Brotherly Love Explained and Enforc'd" (Annapolis, Md.: Green, 1750), pp. 23–27, given in Lemay, *Men of Letters*, pp. 239–40.

48. Lemay, *Men of Letters*, p. 188.

49. Joseph Towne Wheeler, "Reading and Other Recreations of Marylanders, 1700–1776," *Maryland Historical Magazine* 38 (1943): 42–43; Elaine G. Breslaw, "Dr. Alexander Hamilton and the Enlightenment in Maryland" (Ph.D. diss., University of Maryland, 1973), pp. 141–43.

50. *Maryland Gazette*, July 15, 1746.

51. Ibid., Mar. 30, 1748.

52. Hamilton, "History" 1 : 68.

53. Ibid., pp. 85–86.

54. Alexander Hamilton, *Itinerarium, Being a Narrative of a Journey from Annapolis, Maryland through Delaware, Pennsylvania, New York, New Jersey, Connecticut, Rhode Island, Massachusetts and New Hampshire from May to September 1744*, ed. Albert Bushnell Hart (St. Louis: Bixby, 1907), p. 50.

55. Breslaw, ed., *Records*, sederunt 1, May 14, 1745.

56. Hamilton, *Itinerarium*, pp. 186–87.

57. Ibid., p. 234.

58. See Charles Hamm, *Music in the New World* (New York: W. W. Norton, 1983), pp. 38–44.

59. Henry Callister, letter to Anthony Bacon, Oct. 21, 1747, Callister Papers, Maryland Diocesan Archives, Baltimore. "Sanby" was William Sandby, fl. 1742–68, who produced *A Set of New Psalm Tunes and Anthems, in Four Parts . . . the Second Edition, Corrected* (London, 1743); Charles Humphries and William C. Smith, *Music Publishing in the British Isles from the Beginning until the Middle of the Nineteenth Century*, 2d ed. (New York: Barnes and Noble, 1970), p. 285, states that Sandby's psalm collection was advertised in a London newspaper. "J. Robinson" was probably Jacob Robinson, a London publisher who printed music between 1742 and 1758, but may have been John Robinson (ca. 1682–1762), organist at Westminster Abbey, teacher and church music composer. "Heaven open to all men" was probably a collection of psalms or hymns. This order was likely placed on behalf of the Reverend Thomas Bacon, considering the ecclesiastical nature of the selections;

furthermore, Callister implied in various letters that his own interest in the church was somewhat casual.

60. Hamm, *Music in the New World*, pp. 24–47. Most of the documentation for Hamm's chapter on colonial church music is based on New England sources; however, he contends that Anglican church music was much the same in the southern colonies. Certainly, Malcolm's arrival in Annapolis from Massachusetts placed a knowledgeable New England musician in the Maryland capital during the period encompassed by this study.

61. Although no local church records include information about sacred music in this era, the *Maryland Gazette* confirms that at least one psalm tune was known to the general public, for on May 4, 1748, it displayed a song that may be "Sung to the tune of the 119th Psalm." The *Maryland Gazette* of Sept. 6, 1759, requested subscribers "for purchasing an ORGAN for the Church of Annapolis" to pay their promised donations; "St. Anne's Parish Vestry Minutes, 1713–1767," p. 353, Maryland Hall of Records, Annapolis, Md. (microfilm Ms. 1156), contains the following resolution from the vestry meeting of June 29, 1761: "It was unanimously agreed, That an Organ Loft should be Erected in the new Addition of the Church, whereon to fix the Organ lately brought in from England, for the Use of the Church."

3

MUSIC IN ANNAPOLIS

Musicians

During the Tuesday Club era amateur musicians permeated every level of colonial Annapolitan society. Three runaway slaves were among the earliest American performers to be identified by name when rewards for their return were offered in the *Maryland Gazette*. One such notice appeared on September 6, 1745: "Run away . . . from the Head of South River . . . a Mulatto Man John Stokes, alias Collins, aged about 28 years . . . plays very well on the Fiddle and formerly belonged to Dr. Charles Carroll of Annapolis. [Signed] Stephen Higgins." "Toby," a slave belonging to Cornelius Harkins of Kent County, ran away in the spring of 1748, taking with him "a new fiddle, a Bonja, on both which he sometimes plays."[1] "Bonja," as well as "banger" and "banga," were common eighteenth-century names for the banjo. "Prince," a twenty-five-year-old slave who also played the "banger," reportedly absconded with a fiddle during the summer of 1749.[2]

Henry Callister was an Eastern Shore merchant and representative of Robert Morris, father of the famous financier of the American Revolution. Callister provided this insight into the musicians of his social class in a letter to William Tear, dated November 5, 1745: "I have had the pleasure of playing a tune with Bill Stephens, he has lost a great deal of his Musical Capacity, however his performance was found sufficient to ravish and surprise some of our best top Men: You must know we abound in Fidlers but most wretched ones they are—some of the better sort have a little of the true taste, but they are content if they exceed the vulgar in that, & I seldom get any further."[3]

Although Callister was not an Annapolitan, his voluminous correspondence made frequent reference to musical activities in the Chesapeake region, including musicians who performed in Annapolis. He was a guest of the Tuesday Club and was intimately acquainted with several of its musical members, both the Reverend Thomas Bacon and Colonel Edward Lloyd, as well as his own employer, Robert Morris. In 1748 Bacon wrote to Callister: "We are so improved in good company & music that it is worth-while to spend an evening with us. I shall be at the chappel next Sunday, when I hope to see you, and probably fix a day for meeting at Col. Lloyd's to try over the music he has got in."[4] Bacon's friendship with Callister proved to be an enduring one. In 1755 he invited Callister for another evening of music with Colonel Samuel Chamberlaine and Charles Love, an accomplished professional musician; for that occasion, Bacon requested that Callister bring the "Tenor Fiddle," probably referring to a viola da gamba.[5] This foursome appears in later correspondence as "the Musical Society," an indication that their music making was not a rare occurrence.[6]

The estate inventories of Anne Arundel County for the years 1746 through 1759 (see table 2) suggest other performers who may have been active during the Tuesday Club years; at least, it is known they did own musical instruments.

It should be noted that table 2 is limited to probable musicians who died during the period encompassed by this study; certainly others who did not die between 1746 and 1759 were also performing, such as the Tuesday Club musicians. Instruments appeared with increasing frequency in the inventories that followed the Tuesday Club era, and some of the families whose estates were examined in the years 1760–75 included amateur musicians also active during the middle years of the eighteenth century. Furthermore, the evidence of musical instruments in the Tuesday Club documents, in Henry Callister's papers, and in the *Maryland Gazette* indicates that many instruments were never inventoried at all and suggests the existence of a musical community whose numbers substantially exceeded those who could be identified by name.

Two musicians whose music making was at least semiprofessional were George Downey (see p. 16) and John Lammond, who advertised his services in the *Maryland Gazette* of November 28, 1750: "John Lammond, Musician at the house of John Lansdale, Shoemaker in Annapolis, Hereby gives Notice, That if any Gentleman should want Music to their Balls or Merry-Making, upon Application made, they shall be diligently waited on by Their humble servant, John Lammond."[7] Lammond must have been successful in marketing his services; the Masonic lodge of Leonardtown, Maryland, "ordered that John Lemon [*sic*] be paid for his services as fiddler for this Evening Fifteen Shillings current Money and his Itinerant Charges."[8] There is little doubt that "John Lemon" was John Lammond, the Annapolitan. He was the only musician to advertise his services in the *Gazette* during this period; moreover, the likelihood of two itinerant musicians bearing such similar names is small indeed.

TABLE 2

Musical Instruments Inventoried in
Anne Arundel County Estates, 1746–59

Estate	Instrument(s)	Liber : folio	Date
Gassaway Watkins	violin	33 : 282	1746
Samuel Stringer	violins, flute	36 : 44	1747
John Burle	flute	38 : 109	1749
David Stewart	violin	39 : 148	1749
Thomas Joyce	violin	43 : 68	1749
Alexander Warfield	violin	43 : 481	1750
George Downey	2 violins	48 : 148	1750
William Peele	trumpet	60 : 209	1750
Henry Hill	flute	63 : 208	1752
Richard Warfield	violin	54 : 32	1753
Benjamin Warfield	violin, flute	54 : 259	1753
Vincent Dorsey	violin	55 : 244	1753
John Gardener	violin	60 : 513	1755
John Brown	violin	61 : 226	1755
William Ridgly	violin	60 : 685	1756
John Conner	violin	63 : 194	1756
Levin Laurence	violin	64 : 504	1757
Richard Taylor	violin	65 : 527	1758
Sarah Gresham	spinet	69 : 22	1758
John Raitt	violin	69 : 1	1759
Nicholas Watkins	violin	69 : 24	1759

Source: National Endowment for the Humanities, grant no. 0067-79-0738, Nancy Baker, compiler; data currently housed by Historic Annapolis, Inc., 194 Prince George Street, Annapolis, Md. 21401. This grant has supported a detailed analysis of all Anne Arundel County estate inventories of the colonial period. On completion of the project the information will be accessible through a computerized data retrieval system.

John Ormsby, the dancing master whose advertisements appeared in the *Maryland Gazette* of August and October 1757, employed a "Musician who Teaches to play well upon the Violin"[9] and may have been a violinist himself. His manuscript book of fifty-five minuets is an invaluable source for mid-century dance repertoire (see p. 31). The script used in the titles of each minuet appears to match that of the autograph inscription on the flyleaf—"*Ex Libris* / Johannis Ormsby / Annapolis / January the 30th: 1758"—and the minuets themselves are copied in the same hand.[10] The manuscript was carefully executed, presumably by Ormsby; it is unlikely that a skilled colonial copyist would not be an accomplished performer as well.

Contemporaneous accounts of the many balls held in Annapolis make no specific mention of musicians, records of the early Masonic lodge have been lost, and even the Tuesday Club documents fail to identify the musicians who played for its dances. In the absence of any evidence to the contrary, the advertisements of Lammond and Ormsby and of Downey's "two penny hops" suggest that these three musicians may have provided much of the music for dancing in colonial Annapolis.

Two professional musicians also visited mid-century Annapolis. In a letter to Henry Callister, Thomas Bacon related his encounter with John Palma of Philadelphia: "We had on Friday & Saturday last at Col. Lloyd's the most delightful concert America can afford. My Honr. the B[ass?] Fiddle being accompanied on the Harpsichord by the famous Signr. Palma who really is a thorough Master on that Instrumt. and his Execution surprizing. . . . He returns this Week to the Colonel's from Annapolis."[11] Palma was a prominent colonial musician; the *Pennsylvania Gazette* of January 20, 1757, states: "By Particular Desire on Tuesday next, the 25th instant, at the Assembly Room in Lodge Alley will be performed a Concert of Music, under the direction of Mr. John Palma."[12] Another concert, on March 25, 1757, was probably attended by George Washington.[13]

The second professional visitor, Charles Love, had been the harpsichordist for Lewis Hallam's theatrical company when it played in New York in 1753.[14] He performed in the Tuesday Club as a violinist on May 27, 1755, playing the "Quaker Sermon," and was "Mons de L'Amour" in Bacon's letter to Callister of April 3, 1756.[15] This versatile musician also played "all Wind Instruments" and taught dancing and fencing.[16] Love must have enjoyed a considerable reputation as a performer; his name appears in one of New York's earliest concert advertisements:

> For the benefit of Mr. Charles Love, at the New Exchange Ball Room, on Thursday the 24th instant, will be a *Concert* of vocal and instrumental Musick. To which will be added several select pieces on the hautboy, by Mr. Love. After the concert will be a *Ball*. Tickets at 5 s each, to be head of Mr. Love; at the King's Arms; and at Parker's and Gaine's printing office. Tickets given out last summer by Mr. Love, will be taken that night. Mr. Love hopes that gentlemen and ladies will favour him with their good company.[17]

The "vocal music" in the above notice may have been performed by Love's wife, who was a singer in Hallam's company.[18]

After leaving Maryland Charles Love continued south to Westmoreland County, Virginia, where he found employment for a brief time at Stratford, home of Philipp Ludwell Lee. Hallam's former harpsichordist proved to be light-fingered in more ways than one; according to an advertisement placed in several colonial newspapers, he stole his patron's prize bassoon and headed for Charleston, South Carolina.[19]

Many Tuesday Club members and guests were active musicians. Club documents reveal that everyone sang songs; Bacon played the violin and viola da gamba, Robert Morris, the violin; Daniel Wolstenholme was a flutist, Hamilton, a cellist; Alexander Malcolm played both the flute and violin; Daniel Dulany, Jr., and John Wollaston, the painter, were both violinists; Jonas Green played the French horn; and William Lux performed on the organ and harpsichord.[20] William Thornton, the club's "musician con voce" (singer) may also have been a violinist of sorts. In the Tuesday Club record of February 13, 1750, Hamilton accused him of exceeding the bounds of his office for attempting to "play the fiddle." An unidentified drummer completes the Tuesday Club ensemble. Assuredly, other members were musically inclined. Edward Lloyd was known to have ordered music (see p. 25), and James Holliday, "Joshua Fluter," may have been a flutist; however, there is no evidence that they actually performed at club meetings.[21]

It might appear that Annapolis in those middle years of the eighteenth century boasted an unusually active musical life. While such a level of activity may have been remarkable for an American city, music making in the Maryland capital, at least among its upper social classes, was typical of contemporary British society. In describing the rococo style of 1725–60, Homer Ulrich writes in his modern study of chamber music: "Every gentleman played the violin, and every lady the flute. This invasion of music by the amateur in search of diversion required a type of music that was within the technical and intellectual limits of the dilettante. . . ."[22] The musicians of Annapolis substantiate Ulrich's retrospective view of the period.

Instruments

The violin was clearly the favorite instrument—"We abound in fiddlers," wrote Callister—but the flute was also very popular.[23] Bacon's viola da gamba, Hamilton's cello, and Green's French horn were unique in the records of musical Annapolis. The bassoon was probably also heard; Hamilton's account of the lineage of the Tuesday Club states that Mr. George Neilson, president and founder of the Red House Club, an earlier organization, played

> Several instruments, such as the violin, Bass viol, flute, Hautboy and Bassoon, and some say he handled the Jews Harp with great dexterity; but the Bassoon excelled all his other performances, for by means of this solemn instrument, he used to draw many of the Rustics about his door, who flocked to the sound, as the stones and trees did of old to the sound of Orpheus's Harp, with this difference, that, as the harp of the latter

used to animate inanimate beings, so vice versa, the Bassoon of the first, used to inanimate animated beings, or convert human shapes into Sticks and Stones.[24]

While this extraordinary range of abilities is improbable, to say the least, Hamilton's satirical mixture of fact and fiction suggests that the bassoon was indeed familiar to the ears of Marylanders; furthermore, the Reverend John Hamilton, a Tuesday Club member (no relation to Alexander), owned a bassoon, as did Philipp Lee and, subsequently, Charles Love.[25]

All the instruments mentioned in the preceding paragraph were present in Maryland, possibly, during the Tuesday Club years; a "hoe-boy pipe" had been inventoried as early as 1676,[26] and Henry Callister, in 1765, had acquired from Alexander Hamilton's estate a cello, flute, and "Hautbois and reeds."[27] William Peele's trumpet (see table 2) completes the list of wind instruments that can be placed in mid-century Annapolis.

The banjo, as noted at the beginning of this chapter, was popular in Annapolis and throughout the colonies, particularly among the slaves. In 1781 Thomas Jefferson wrote: "The instrument proper to them is the *banjar* which they brought from Africa and which is the original of the guitar, its chords being precisely the four lower chords of the guitar."[28] The availability of other members of the lute-guitar family is uncertain. Bacon wrote to Callister, "Your strum-strum must wait til the garden will permit me a day or two's leisure to tinkle it at Oxford," but the instrument is not otherwise identified.[29]

Keyboard instruments were also available. Although St. Anne's Church, the most important house of worship in eighteenth-century Annapolis,[30] did not acquire an organ until the 1760s, harpsichords and organs were known to have existed in the city. John Stevenson advertised an "Organ and spinnet from Germany" for sale in the *Maryland Gazette* of November 21, 1754, and Tuesday Club records show that William Lux played an organ and harpsichord at the house of Thomas Jennings and an organ at John Bullen's home.[31] Jonas Green advertised "a very good spinnet to be disposed of. Enquire of the Printer," in his *Gazette* of June 30, 1747, and Sarah Gresham's estate included a spinet in 1758. On the Eastern Shore a harpsichord was reported in the home of Edward Lloyd (see p. 27), and Thomas Bacon's estate inventory included "an old harpsichord."[32] Thomas Richison's dulcimer accompanied Hamilton's cello in a Tuesday Club sederunt of November 21, 1752.[33] Although not a keyboard instrument, the dulcimer is generally regarded as a forerunner of the modern piano, insofar as its strings were struck by hand-held hammers.

Military drums and an eighteenth-century oddity, "Eight musical bells rung by an electrified Phial," possibly a form of glass harmonica, complete the catalog of musical instruments.[34]

Repertoire

The music of the ballad operas produced in Annapolis during the period covered by this study forms the largest body of songs whose performances can be documented. Although the extent of their popularity is difficult to ascertain, at least a few of the songs were performed independently, such as "Whilst I Gaze on Chloe, Trembling" and the air "Come Jolly Bacchus," both from *The Devil to Pay* (see chap. 2) and both sung in the Tuesday Club.[35] The estate of Robert Morris included a copy of *The Beggar's Opera* with several other unidentified plays, and the Reverend James Sterling was familiar with the work, having been the husband of a leading Polly Peachum.[36] Considering the participation of "Private Gentlemen" in the Upper Marlborough *Beggar's Opera*, it can be stated with a reasonable degree of certainty that the songs of *The Beggar's Opera* were well known to local musicians. (A complete listing of song titles from the Annapolis season is presented in appendix A.)

A major source of printed secular music was the *Gentleman's Magazine*, published in London and widely circulated in the American colonies. Each monthly issue from 1745 through 1755 usually featured one or two songs or dances with music. Contributors to this popular periodical included established composers such as George Frideric Handel, William Boyce, Thomas Arne, James Oswald, John Stanley, John Frederick Lampe, Samuel Howard, Richard Leveridge, Simon Stubley, and John Alcock; even some gentlemen subscribers were also represented. The magazine's selections reveal a cross-section of British popular music drawn from contemporaneous ballad operas, English and Scots songs, and public garden concerts, as well as new compositions and pieces composed for special occasions. The *Gentleman's Magazine* was well known in Annapolis: Jonas Green reprinted several articles from it in his *Maryland Gazette*, and copies of the actual magazine are found in the inventories of several colonial libraries. Henry Callister ordered the magazine from Anthony Bacon, brother of his friend Thomas Bacon, in 1749; Charles Carroll, the barrister, wrote for "a Complete set of Gentleman's Magazine from as far back as you can get them to the present time," in 1756.[37] One of the Tuesday Club songs, "Bumpers Squire Jones," appeared in the November 1744 issue; another club song, "Stand Round My Brave Boys," by George Frideric Handel, was printed in the *London Magazine* of November 1745.[38] Both "magazine" songs were sung in club on the same evening by John Lomas, a possible subscriber.[39]

The dances of the *Gentleman's Magazine* are particularly enlightening for what they suggest about performance practice: all are scored for solo violin, and most contain instructions for executing the dance steps. The extent to which the magazine music was actually used cannot be documented; however, the music was present in Annapolis, and it represented a likely source of secular composition, considering both the scarcity of American music publications and the relative difficulty of obtaining specific scores from the British Isles.[40] (Songs and dances contained in the *Gentleman's Magazine*, 1744 through 1755, are listed in appendix B.)

John Ormsby's manuscript collection of fifty-five minuets, dated 1758, is the only set of dances that can be placed in Annapolis in the 1750s.[41] Like the dances in the *Gentleman's Magazine*, Ormsby's minuets are scored for solo violin. The principal composers represented are "Signior Martini," "Giminiani [*sic*]," "Mr. Handel," "Corelli," "Gardini [*sic*]," "Signior Lacatelli [*sic*]," and "The Reverd. Mr. Bacon."[42] Several minuets are titled for prominent personages, for example, "Lord Glenorche's Minuet" and "Lady Roshe's Minuet";[43] some bear the names of ladies and gentlemen prominent in Maryland society, such as "Miss Chase" and "Col. Tasker."[44] Ormsby's misspellings may indicate that the music was copied from memory rather than from published sources; the execution of the manuscript is otherwise meticulous. As a dancing master Ormsby advertised his services for Baltimore and Upper Marlborough.[45] His collection of minuets was probably widely used in Maryland, both for dance instruction and for balls or merrymaking.

British ballads and Scots songs were popular. Although no published collections of such music have been discovered in the records of mid-eighteenth-century Annapolis, knowledge of collections containing songs performed in the Tuesday Club is useful in identifying a body of secular vocal music that may have been familiar to Marylanders of this period. These songs and their sources will be described in detail in chapter 4. Collections featuring several of the club songs include *The Muses Delight* (Liverpool: John Sadler, 1754) and *Calliope* (London: Henry Roberts, 1739 [vol. 1] and 1746 [vol. 2]). A third collection, *Musick for Allan Ramsay's Collection of Scots Songs*, was ordered by Henry Callister in 1744: "I want Allen Ramsay's Songs, which your friend the Bookseller may get you, I want the complete Sett of Musick and all the Songs . . . [which] will be in one small volume and the Airs in 2 or 3 small octavos or 12's."[46] It is not certain whether Callister ever received the volume he requested; however, in a letter from Thomas Bacon, Callister was asked to "send the book of songs,"[47] and "Auld Rob Morris," cited in Hamilton's history, is included in this collection.[48]

While it cannot be proved that other songs of these collections were sung in Annapolis, it can be stated that such publications represent a genre enjoyed by Marylanders of this period. (Appendix C comprises a partial listing of contemporaneous collections of English ballads and Scots songs.)

In addition to songs of the British Isles, rounds and catches were also popular. Two that appear in Tuesday Club documents may be found in modern collections, but no contemporaneous sources for rounds and catches of eighteenth-century Annapolis have come to light. Such repertoire was most often produced by clubs devoted to the composing and performing of various canons and glees. Although a few outstanding works by such composers as Henry Purcell, John Blow, and John Hilton were printed, the bulk of catches and rounds by musical amateurs was never published. Bacon probably belonged to one such club, Dublin's Hibernian Catch Club, which was founded in 1679 and claims to be the oldest music society in Europe.[49]

The principal collections of catches popular in England during the Tuesday Club period were *The Second Book of the Pleasant Musical Companion*, 9th ed. (London: Playford, 1726), *The Pleasant Musical Companion*, 10th ed. (London: Playford, 1730), *The Catch Club, or Merry Companions* (London: Walsh, ca. 1730), and *The Pleasant Musical Companion* (Cheapside: Johnson, ca. 1740), the last being a reprint of the two earlier Playford compilations. *The Gentleman's Catch Book* (Dublin: Mountain, 1786) is a compilation of favorite catches of the Hibernian Catch Club; if the inclusion on page 25 of the catch by "The Reverend Mr. Bacon" indicates that Bacon had been a member of the catch club while in Dublin, then this collection contains catches and rounds known to him, and possibly known to his Maryland friends as well.

Masonic songsters included some of the earliest song texts printed in America. Although no records exist of their use in Annapolis, considering both the musical abilities of the leaders in the Annapolis lodge of the 1750s and the musical traditions of the Freemasons, it is reasonable to assume that Masonic songs were sung. The *Maryland Gazette*'s advertisement of *The Beggar's Opera* to be presented at Upper Marlborough in 1752 included a notice that Mr. Woodham would sing a "Mason's Song . . . with a Grand Chorus."[50] The first song to be documented in Maryland's Masonic records is the "Entered Apprentice's Song," sung in the Leonardtown lodge in the early 1760s.[51] Irving Lowens's study *A Bibliography of Songsters Printed in America before 1821*, which appeared in 1976, includes only one songster produced prior to the Tuesday Club period: *The Constitution of the Free-Masons*, reprinted in 1734 by Benjamin Franklin. An extant copy now owned by the University of Pennsylvania contains twenty-seven manuscript tunes for Masonic songs in addition to its five printed song texts.[52] The Philadelphia printer was well known in Annapolis; he placed a notice in the *Maryland Gazette* of 1754 announcing his trip to Maryland as postmaster general, visited the Tuesday Club during his stay, and was not only a colleague but a friend of Jonas Green.[53] His songster may well be a source of Annapolis Masonic music. *The American Mock Bird* of 1760 contains a much more extensive repertoire of 336 songs. Printed in New York City for James Rivington and sold at his warehouse in Philadelphia,[54] this collection surely contains songs enjoyed by American and possibly Annapolis Freemasons during the 1750s.

Townspeople also composed songs. The *Maryland Gazette* of September 19, 1754, included the words of "A Recruiting Song, For the Maryland Independent Company," composed by an officer of the company; unfortunately, no tune was suggested.[55] Tuesday Club songs attest to the practice of writing song texts to be set to existing tunes, although occasionally original melodies such as Cole's tune for the musical mock trial of Thomas King were also composed.[56]

In the absence of readily available printed music, hand-copied songsters were common. One such book, now in the Diocesan Archives of Baltimore, contains a favorite song of the Tuesday Club. Handel's "Stand Round My Brave Boys" appears in this songster copied in several hands, circa 1751. The manuscript's provenance is uncertain, but the songs were probably set down in colonial Maryland. Charles Cole carried a songster in his pocket, "he having a number of old songs by him, to the words of which, he affirms, he never is at a loss to find a tune."[57] One popular song of the day, "Tune of a Cobler There Was, He Lived in a Stall," was even found copied in an account book:

> Some Coblers turn poets to serve their Just Friends
> Some Members turn Coblers to Serve there by ends
> Good Lord what mean notions in these Members lurk
> To Rob a Poor Cobler of all Cobling work
>   Sing derry down down down,
>   derry down

The song consists of ten verses with refrain.[58]

Instrumentalists also drew heavily from the repertoire of the British Isles, including both traditional folk music and the works of major European composers published in London. Henry Callister wrote in 1745 that, "as to other English tunes, they murther [*sic*] them here ten times worse then the Country Fidlers [*sic*] of the Island [The Isle of Man]."[59] Hamilton wrote of one club meeting: "After supper was played the Grand Chorus of 1751 . . . and several pieces of the celebrated Vivaldi."[60] Callister assessed the value of some music that he had loaned to a friend as follows: "I would sooner part with the whole works of Corelli, than lose it."[61] Jonas Green's poem describing a particularly festive evening in the Tuesday Club alluded to books of "Corelli, Vivaldi, Alberti, and others."[62] Hamilton, writing on the decline of the Romans, mentioned performers as well as composers: "Signior Corelli, Vivaldi, Tessarini, Torelli, Martini, Geminiani, Alberti, Valentini, Lampugnani, Senesino, Farinello, Bonancini, Beneditto, and Seniora or Madona Auretti, Violante, Berberini &ct."[63]

The Ormsby manuscript supports the popularity of the Italians, with tunes of Corelli, Martini, Geminiani, Giardini, and Locatelli, as well as Handel (see p. 31), whose British reputation was derived first from his prowess as a composer of Italian operas and later from his English oratorios. (Handel's German contemporaries J. S. Bach, Telemann, Quantz, and others were relatively unknown in mid-eighteenth-century Annapolis.) Handel was revered by Tuesday Club musicians; his name appears in the dedication of Malcolm's *Treatise*, and Thomas Bacon was impressed by the premiere of Handel's *Messiah* (see pp. 54–55). Both from the preceding and from other references, we know that the works of serious composers were available in Annapolis. Thomas Bacon owned a superior music collection. According to Callister, "I should have passed for a tip top musician if the Revd. Mr. Bacon had not come in. . . . He is a very agreeable Companion, is a sober & learned man. His performance of the violin and violoncello have afforded me much delight. I have a pretty sett of Musick & he has still a better."[64]

It is indeed unfortunate that the music owned by Bacon, Callister, and their Maryland contemporaries was never inventoried. Such a survey was made of the music owned by Cuthbert Ogle of Williamsburg, who died in 1755.[65] From a cultural, economic, and social point of view, Annapolis resembled Williamsburg more closely than any other colonial capital. The social activities of the Virginia city were well publicized in the *Maryland Gazette* of the time; Bacon was invited there to preach and to perform a benefit concert where he surely enjoyed some contact with Virginian musicians.[66] Although the Ogle repertoire cannot be placed in Annapolis, it does reveal a selection of British and European art music that was available to colonial musicians of the Tuesday Club years, some of which may have been heard in the Annapolis area and may have been present in Maryland collections as well. Ogle's library included works by Alberti, Alcock, Avison, Burgess, Corbett, Corelli, Giardini, Granom, Handel, Hasse, Hebden, Leveridge, Nares, Pasquali, Purcell, Rameau, Woodward, Lampe, and Palma, all of which were available from British publishing houses, especially Walsh.[67]

It is difficult to assess the significance of the Ogle collection for colonial Virginia; his inventory does reveal the repertoire that this colonial musician thought useful when he advertised his services as a music teacher in the *Virginia Gazette* of March 28, 1755. The inventory further lists specific pieces by composers whose names appear in Annapolis documents, particularly works by the Italian composers Corelli, Alberti, Giardini, and Pasquali.

Virtually all the string players in the Tuesday Club were educated in the British Isles. Hamilton and Malcolm emigrated from Edinburgh; Daniel Dulany, Jr., and John Wollaston were trained in London; and Bacon spent several years in Dublin, where, as publisher of the *Dublin Mercury* (Jan. 1742–Sept. 1742) and the *Dublin Gazette* (Sept. 1742–July 1743), he may have witnessed performances by Handel, Arne, Domenico Scarlatti, and Geminiani.[68] These Tuesday Club players all had the means and the musical ability to absorb much from British concert life; they surely must have brought their favorite pieces of music from the British capitals to their new homes in America.

A few compositions that appear in the Callister papers suggest possible American origins: "Chicomocomoco" and "Johnny Boy" were identified as "the music that is most relished here."[69] Charles Love's "Quaker Sermon," performed in the Tuesday Club in July 1755, may also be of colonial origin. However, no serious researcher could dismiss the Tuesday Club repertoire as "contemporary folk music of colonial Maryland."[70] The repertoire of colonial Annapolis in general, and of the Tuesday Club in particular, was cosmopolitan in every respect, reflecting the musical tastes of eighteenth-century London, Dublin, and Edinburgh in its popular songs and dances, its favorite Italian composers, and in the music composed by the Tuesday Club musicians.

Instructional Material

Instructional materials that can be placed in Maryland are Christopher Simpson's *Principles of Practicle Musick* (London, 1665), Alexander Malcolm's *Treatise of Musick* (Edinburgh, 1721), and possibly William Tans'ur's *New Musical Grammar* (London, 1746).[71]

Thomas Bacon must have developed some of his skill as a composer from studying Simpson's work. He recommended it to Callister in January 1746: "I sent you Si——pson's Compendium which you will find easy & at the same time full enough for any young student in composition."[72]

Malcolm's own treatise received international acclaim; it displays extensive familiarity with earlier theorists, including Pythagoras and Guido of Arezzo, and quotes Aristotle, Seneca, and Cassiodorus in their original Greek or Latin.[73] Malcolm was familiar with Etienne Loulié's studies of pendulum metronomes in *Elements ou principes de musique* (Paris: Christophe Ballard, 1696) and was among the earliest theorists to describe equal temperament (although he did not actually advocate the system, as Fuller-Maitland claimed in *The Oxford History of Music*).[74] For Maryland musicians his treatise was useful as a guide to tuning harpsichords, and it included a brief, but lucid, section on harmony and counterpoint with musical examples. His rules are well within the common practice of the early eighteenth century, excepting the prohibition of certain chord inversions and interval successions, possibly imposed to avoid dissonances created by the system of just intonation.[75]

Malcolm's *Treatise* was widely distributed in America. Newport's Redwood Library and Athenaeum (established 1747) had a copy in its original collection,[76] as did Robert Carter of Nomini Hall, Virginia.[77] Maryland's Henry Callister owned a copy, which he misplaced: "I cannot find Malcolm's treatise; I suppose I have lent it out somewhere."[78] Callister also ordered Tans'ur's *New Musical Grammar* from Anthony Bacon.[79] It is difficult to gauge the influence of these treatises on local composers; Bacon's work was probably guided by Simpson's instruction, and Malcolm himself was a compositional force in the club. The significant point is that Annapolis composers had access to at least two of the most important theoretical works of their time.

Performances

Public concerts were infrequent during the Tuesday Club years. Only five such programs appear in contemporaneous records, four of which were announced in the *Maryland Gazette*. The first concert of this era was a performance of the Tuesday Club anniversary ode of 1751, which took place on May 14, 1751. Hamilton's description of the occasion follows:

> The Grand procession arrived at the Council Chamber where the music of the anniversary ode, Composed by Signior Lardini [Bacon], a worthy honorary member of the Club, was performed on many Instruments accompanied with voices, with great applause, before a grand and Splendid assembly of the prime Gentlemen and Ladies, to whom the poet Laureat [Green] presented printed Copies of the ode; Signior Lardini play'd the violino primo, The Chancellor [Malcolm], violino Secondo, Signior Giovanni Preciso [Daniel Wolstenholme], a Gentleman Invited to the Club performed the flauto part, the Secretary [Hamilton] the Bass, and Mr. John Gabble [John Bacon] of the Eastern Shore Triumvirate executed the vocal part, with an excellent good Grace; for which good performance, his Lordship the president afterwards Said, that that young Gentleman deserved to be made a Bishop.[80]

The first *Maryland Gazette* concert notice appeared on October 2, 1751: "This evening will be performed, by a Set of Gentlemen, a Concert of Music, in the Council Chamber, for the Benefit of the Talbot County Charity School." The "Set of Gentlemen" at this concert was to include Tuesday Club members. The establishing of the Talbot County Charity School was Bacon's project; moreover, the club's record for October 8, 1751, noted that the meeting was a week late because "of the necessary attendance of Several of the members of this Club, at a rehearsal of music for a charitable Concert, performed on Wednesday night last."[81] The program is unknown but may well have included the 1751 ode; numerous entries in both the history and records attest to its in-club popularity (see p. 116). Later, a second benefit concert was held in Upper Marlborough, in the "Great Ball Room," again for the Talbot County Charity School.[82] This concert, advertised for October 19, 1752, probably featured Bacon and his Tuesday Club friends.

Yet another Upper Marlborough concert was advertised in the *Maryland Gazette* for June of the next year: "Upon Thursday the 28th of this Instant June, will be performed at Upper Marlborough; a grand Concert of Music, with many Instruments, in the Ball Room: The Evening will be concluded with a Ball. Tickets may be had at Mr. Benjamin Barry's, Mr. Benjamin Brooke's, and at Mrs. Hillary's, in Marlborough."[83] Neither the performers nor the program was identified, so it is not definitely known whether or not Tuesday Club members participated. It is believed that they had been involved with *The Beggar's Opera* performance in Upper Marlborough, given during the preceding September.

The fifth concert recorded in the *Maryland Gazette* of this era occurred in Williamsburg and was yet another benefit performance for Bacon's charity school. The notice of December 19, 1754, advised readers that the Virginia benefactors had raised twelve pounds, two shillings, nine pence for Bacon's school, "On account of a concert of Music in the College Hall." The concert had taken place in November. Bacon may have performed; he had promoted his school by performing and preaching in Williamsburg on earlier occasions.[84]

These concerts are notable in the annals of American music. They are remarkable for their antiquity and for their being among the first public performances of music actually composed in America.

This was an era of solo and chamber music. The largest ensemble to perform in Annapolis was probably the Tuesday Club's instrumentalists, a group that did not exceed seven players, at least not in any documented performance.[85] Ensembles of two to four players are frequently mentioned in Callister's correspondence and in Tuesday Club documents, but the dominant instrumental combination of the period was the trio. The Tuesday Club instrumental music and anniversary odes were typically scored for two treble instruments and one bass part, with the vocal part doubling one of the treble lines. From numerous club accounts it is obvious that the odes were performed by whomever was available to play and sing. Many parts were doubled, some occasionally omitted.[86] Considering the range and difficulty of the vocal writing, it is likely that the voice part was doubled by a flute or violin. Since many of the florid vocal passages are textually repetitious, an instrument could have been substituted without significantly altering the musical sense.

An unusual aspect of Annapolis music, at least for present-day listeners, is the performance of unaccompanied solo vocal and instrumental music. Many accounts of club singing suggest that this was standard practice.[87] English songsters of the era and many editions of ballad operas were often printed with only a melody line (see, for example, John Ormsby's book of minuets), while Henry Callister's letters suggest solo violin playing, albeit of questionable quality: it bears repeating that he considered the players generally "wretched" and their musical treatment of good "English tunes" tantamount to murder.[88] John Lammond's notice in the *Maryland Gazette* and an expense item from the records of the Leonardtown Masonic lodge further support the notion that "Music to their Balls and Merry-Making" was often provided by one "Fidler."[89]

There were no standing ensembles with fixed combinations of instruments. Annapolis was fortunate indeed to have players of sufficient numbers, skill, and interest, as well as with enough leisure time, to produce an active musical society capable of presenting public concerts and private entertainments. It is notable that the promoters (Green and his *Maryland Gazette*), sponsors (Freemasons and benefactors of the Talbot County Charity School), and performers in some of America's earliest public concerts were members of the same club and often the same people. Their names appear, with their club pseudonyms, in table 3.

TABLE 3
Members of the Tuesday Club
(listed in order of admission)

Member	Pseudonym	Admitted
Robert Gordon[a]	Capt. Serious Social	1745
William Rogers[a]	Capt. Seemly Spruce	1745
Rev. John Gordon[a,b]	Rev. Smoothum Sly	1745
William Cumming, Sr.[a]	Jealous Spyplot	1745
John Bullen[a]	Capt. Bully Blunt	1745
	Sir John Oldcastle	
John Lomas[a]	Laconic Comus	1745
Witham Marshe[a]	Prattle Motely	1745
Dr. Alexander Hamilton[a]	Loquatious Scribble	1745
James Calder[b]	Abraham Bumper	1745
Mark Gibson	Dumpling Gundiguts	1745
Charles Cole	Carlos Nasifer Jole	1745
George Atkinson	Joggle Hasty	1745
Edward Dorsey	Drawlum Quaint	1745
Walter Dulany	Slyboots Pleasant	1745
Dr. John Hamilton[b]	Dr. Polyhistor	1745
Col. Edward Lloyd[b]	Col. Courtly Phraze	1745
William Thornton	Protomusicus	1745
	Solo Neverout	
Rev. Thomas Bacon[b,c]	Signior Lardini	1745
Rev. John Hamilton[c]	Broadface Round	1745
Dr. Robert Holliday[c]	Dr. Hereum Thereum	1745
Richard Snowdon[b]	Oldham Wisley	1745
James Holliday[b]	Joshua Fluter	1745
Robert North[b]	Huffbluff Surly	1745
Samuel Hart[b]	Ignotus Warble	1745
Robert Morris[b,c]	Merry Makefun	1747

TABLE 3 (*continued*)

Member	Pseudonym	Admitted
Richard Hill[b]	Chantum Cheary	1747
Abraham Barnes[b]	Curious Courtly	1747
John Addison[b]	Swillum Swagbelly	1747
Edward Tilghman[b]	Prim Laconic	1747
Jonas Green	Jonathan Grog	1748
Stephen Bordley	Huffman Snap	1749
Beale Bordley	Quirpum Comic	1749
William Cumming, Jr.	Jealous Spyplot, Jr.	1749
Thomas Jennings	Prim Timorous	1749
Rev. Andrew Lendrum	Roundhead Muddy	1749
Rev. Alexander Malcolm	Philo-Dogmaticus	1749
Richard Dorsey	Tunebelly Bowser	1750
James Dickinson[b,c]	Theophilous Smirker	1750
Dennis Dulany[b]	Capt. Dio Ramble	1750
Thomas Cumming[b]	Coney Pimp Frontinbras	1750
John Bacon[b]	John Gabble	1751
William Lux	Crinkum Crankum	1753
Rev. Thomas Cradock	Bard Mevius	1753
Col. William Fitzhugh	Col. Comico Butman	1753
Michael Earle	Jocifer Bluechin	1754
Dr. Upton Scott	Dr. Jeronimo Jaunter	1754

Source: Comparison, by sederunt, of actual names in Breslaw, ed., *Records of the Tuesday Club*, with facetious pseudonyms and membership lists recorded in Hamilton's history. The complete list of Tuesday Club pseudonyms given in Robert J. Micklus, "Dr. Alexander Hamilton's 'History of the Tuesday Club,'" 4 vols. (Ph.D. diss., University of Delaware, 1980), 4:1724–28, does not distinguish between members and guests, but a list of members and guests showing meetings attended may be found in appendix B of Breslaw's edition. The extent to which the pseudonyms were used in club meetings is uncertain. Some, such as "Sir John," "Signior Lardini," and "Protomusicus," appear in the records, but the vast majority of the names do not. The use of pseudonyms based on a person's interests or personal characteristics was a common eighteenth-century literary device that Hamilton probably employed to heighten the humorous effect of his history.

[a] founding members
[b] honorary members
[c] members of Eastern Shore Triumvirate

NOTES

1. *Maryland Gazette*, June 8, 1748.

2. Ibid., Aug. 30, 1749. Dena J. Epstein, *Sinful Tunes and Spirituals: Black Folk Music to the Civil War* (Urbana: University of Illinois Press, 1977), pp. 359–60, provides a list of eighteenth-century names for the banjo.

3. Henry Callister, letter to William Tear, Nov. 5, 1745, Callister Papers, Maryland Diocesan Archives, Baltimore.

4. Thomas Bacon, letter to Henry Callister, May 3, 1748, Callister Papers; Elaine G. Breslaw, ed., *Records of the Tuesday Club of Annapolis, 1745–56* (Urbana: University of Il-

linois Press, 1988), sederunt 32, Apr. 1, 1746, on which date "Callester [*sic*]" visited the club.

5. Thomas Bacon, letter to Henry Callister, n.d. 1755, Callister Papers; Breslaw, ed., *Records*, sederunt 59, May 26, 1747, at which Bacon played a "viol a gamba, or six stringed Bass."

6. Thomas Bacon, letter to Henry Callister, Apr. 3, 1756, Callister Papers.

7. *Maryland Gazette*, Nov. 28, 1750; Jan. 2, 1751.

8. Edward T. Schultz, *History of Freemasonry in Maryland* (Baltimore: Medairy, 1884), 1:30–31, quoting records for Dec. 28, 1761.

9. *Maryland Gazette*, Oct. 20, 1757.

10. Ormsby's manuscript (hereafter referred to as Ormsby MS) is located in the Library and Museum of the Performing Arts, Lincoln Center, New York.

11. Thomas Bacon, letter to Henry Callister, Oct. 26, 1756, Callister Papers. This "Signr. Palma" should not be confused with Filippo Palma, composer and performer, active on the Continent and in England, a contemporary of John Palma. Filippo's songs appear in the Ogle inventory at Williamsburg, but Lemay, *Men of Letters*, stated that the "Palma" songs in the collection of Francis Hopkinson were composed by the Philadelphia Palma. See Maurer Maurer, "The Library of a Colonial Musician, 1755," *William and Mary Quarterly* 7 (1950): 48; J. A. Leo Lemay, *Men of Letters in Colonial Maryland* (Knoxville: University of Tennessee Press, 1972), p. 335n.; Oscar G. T. Sonneck, *Francis Hopkinson . . . and James Lyon* (1905; rpt., New York: Da Capo Press, 1966), p. 33.

12. Oscar G. T. Sonneck, *Early Concert-Life in America (1731–1800)* (1907; rpt., New York: Da Capo Press, 1978), p. 65.

13. Ibid., p. 65, quotes an entry in Washington's ledger, dated Mar. 17, 1757, that shows that Washington had purchased tickets for a Palma concert, probably the performance advertised in the *Pennsylvania Gazette* for Mar. 25, 1757.

14. Ibid., p. 159.

15. Breslaw, ed., *Records*, sederunt 240, May 27, 1755; Thomas Bacon, letter to Henry Callister, Apr. 3, 1756, Callister Papers. Love regularly performed with the Callister-Bacon-Chamberlain ensemble. "You'll not forget that Mr. Ham-on [Hamilton?] expects the Musical Society at his House on Monday. Coll. Chamberlaine I hope has Notice. . . . We shall want what Music you and he have with the Tenor Fiddle (etc.) which please to bring up with you. And Monsr. de L'Amour [Charles Love] must not fail"; in Thomas Bacon, letter to Henry Callister, Oct. 26, 1756, Callister Papers. In another letter, Bacon invited Callister to bring the "Tenor Fiddle" and "Mr. Love," stating further that he would summon Col. Chamberlaine; Thomas Bacon, letter to Henry Callister, n.d. 1755, Callister Papers.

16. Gilbert Chase, *America's Music: From the Pilgrims to the Present*, 2d rev. ed. (New York: McGraw-Hill, 1966), pp. 106–7.

17. *New York Mercury*, Jan. 1754, in Sonneck, *Early Concert-Life*, pp. 159–60. According to Sonneck this was only the fifth concert notice to appear in a New York newspaper.

18. Sonneck, *Early Concert-Life*, p. 159.

19. Chase, *America's Music*, pp. 106–7.

20. Breslaw, ed., *Records*, sederunts 25 and 59, Nov. 26, 1745, and May 26, 1747 (Bacon); sederunt 59, May 26, 1747 (Morris); sederunt 155, May 14, 1751 (Wolstenholme); sederunt 168, Nov. 26, 1751 (Hamilton); sederunt 171, Jan. 7, 1752 (Malcolm); sederunt 171, Jan. 7, 1752 (Dulany); sederunt 202, May 15, 1753 (Wollaston); sederunt 188, Oct. 26, 1752 (Green); sederunt 169, Dec. 10, 1751 (Lux); Alexander Hamilton, *Itinerarium, Being a Narrative of a Journey from Annapolis, Maryland through Delaware, Pennsylvania, New York, New Jersey, Connecticut, Rhode Island, Massachusetts and New Hampshire from May to September 1744*, ed. Albert Bushnell Hart (St. Louis: Bixby, 1907), p. 145 (Malcolm).

21. Lemay, *Men of Letters*, p. 189, states that Samuel Hart played the flute, but Hamilton's reference to Hart's "delicate pipes" probably referred to his voice. Breslaw, ed., *Records*, sederunt 105, May 16, 1749. For a similar reference, see p. 49.

22. Homer Ulrich, *Chamber Music* (New York: Columbia University Press, 1948), p. 115.

23. Henry Callister, letter to William Tear, Nov. 5, 1745, Callister Papers.

24. Alexander Hamilton, "History of the Ancient and Honorable Tuesday Club," 3 vols., The Johns Hopkins University Library and Maryland Historical Society, Baltimore, 1:80–81. Neilson founded the Red House Club in 1728 and was formerly a member of the Whin-bush Club of Edinburgh; Hamilton, "History" 1:68.

25. Joseph Towne Wheeler, "Reading and Other Recreations of Marylanders, 1700–1776," *Maryland Historical Magazine* 38 (1943): 49; Chase, *America's Music*, pp. 106–7.

26. Anne Arundel County Inventories, 1676, in National Endowment for the Humanities, grant no. 0067-79-0738, comp. Nancy Baker.

27. Henry Callister, letter to Dr. Troup, Apr. 2, 1765, Callister Papers.

28. Thomas Jefferson, *Notes on Virginia* [1781] (London: J. Stockdale, 1787); quoted in G. A. Keeler, "Banjo," *Grove's Dictionary of Music and Musicians*, 5th ed. (London: Macmillan, 1954), 1:403. Scholars have disagreed on the origin of the banjo, but recent studies confirm Jefferson's belief that the instrument is African in origin. See Epstein, *Sinful Tunes and Spirituals*, pp. 30–38.

29. Thomas Bacon, letter to Henry Callister, May 12, 1755, Callister Papers. The instrument may have been a banjo; see Epstein, *Sinful Tunes and Spirituals*, pp. 359–60.

30. St. Anne's Church was the city's "established" church, the only church supported by taxation.

31. *Maryland Gazette*, Nov. 21, 1754; Breslaw, ed., *Records*, sederunt 169, Dec. 10, 1751; sederunt 180, May 26, 1752.

32. Frederick County Inventories, 1769, box 6, folder 38.

33. Hamilton, "History" 3:142; Breslaw, ed., *Records*, sederunt 190, Nov. 21, 1752.

34. *Maryland Gazette*, May 10, 1749, reporting a demonstration of properties of electricity given at a house previously occupied by Walter Dulany. In addition to the "musical bells," an "electrified picture" was displayed, possibly the work of Benjamin Franklin, whose interest in electrical experiments as well as glass harmonicas was well known. Franklin visited Annapolis and was known in the Tuesday Club as "Electrico Vitrifico"; see Hamilton, "History" 3:299.

35. Hamilton, "History" 1:162–63; 2:453–54; Breslaw, ed., *Records*, sederunt 24, Nov. 12, 1745; and sederunt 168, Nov. 26, 1751.

36. Wheeler, "Reading and Other Recreations," p. 170; Lemay, *Men of Letters*, p. 259.

37. Henry Callister, letter to Anthony Bacon, Oct. 21, 1749, Callister Papers; Joseph Towne Wheeler, "Reading Interests of Maryland Planters and Merchants, 1700–1776," *Maryland Historical Magazine* 37 (1942): 296, quoting Charles Carroll, letter to William Perkins, Oct. 21, 1756.

38. "Bumpers Squire Jones," *Gentleman's Magazine*, 11 (1744): 612; "Stand Round My Brave Boys," *London Magazine* 11 (1745): 560–61.

39. Hamilton, "History" 1:423; Breslaw, ed., *Records*, sederunt 102, Mar. 21, 1749.

40. Henry Callister expressed concern over the difficulty of replacing some of his music, which had been borrowed: "The Book I want contains select pieces I have myself with some pains collected" (Henry Callister, letter to George Okill, May 1744, Callister Papers), and "I cannot make 'em up without purchasing the whole works of several masters (A thing not to be done in this Country)" (Henry Callister, letter to W. Shepherd, May 1744, Callister Papers). Callister had loaned his music to Shepherd and asked Okill's assistance in retrieving it.

41. Ormsby MS is not a full copybook; the minuets are followed by several blank pages of lined manuscript paper. The dancing master, arriving in Annapolis about 1757, probably began recording the dances that were already popular. It is unlikely he would have encountered Bacon's minuet (the fifth selection) before his arrival in Annapolis. At least some of the minuets had therefore been popular for some time.

42. Giovanni Battista Martini (1706–84), Francesco Geminiani (1687–1762), Felice de' Giardini (1716–96), and Pietro Locatelli (1695–1764).

43. Ormsby MS, pp. 14–15.

44. Ibid., pp. 1, 17. The Chase family was both large and prominent, including more than one "Miss Chase" in 1758; "Col. Benjamin Tasker" was the son of the Annapolis mayor, Benjamin Tasker, and brother-in-law of Governor Ogle. See Aubrey C. Land, *Colonial Maryland* (Millwood, N.Y.: Krause-Thomas, 1981), p. 195.

45. *Maryland Gazette*, Aug. 4, 1757; Oct. 20, 1757.

46. Henry Callister, letter to Mr. Whitfield, Aug. 13, 1744, Callister Papers. *Musick for Allan Ramsay's Collection of Scots Songs* (Edinburgh: Allan Ramsay, [1726]) was the only collection of tunes for Ramsay's poems to be published without text.

47. Thomas Bacon, letter to Henry Callister, Jan. 28, 1746, Callister Papers.

48. Hamilton, "History" 1:160; *Musick for Allan Ramsay's Collection*, pp. 116–17.

49. A catch by Bacon was published in 1786 in a collection of favorite catches of this club; see chap. 5, song 29. The catch is attributed to "The Rev. Mr. Bacon." Bacon was not a clergyman while in Dublin; therefore, the members were aware of his Maryland career. Either Bacon sent them the catch after immigrating to the colonies (unlikely, for why would a Dublin club be interested in the music of an American clergyman?) or he composed it during his Dublin years. If a catch club considered the work of a local composer to be among its favorites, it seems likely that the club would have welcomed that composer as a member, and would have followed his career after his departure from Dublin.

50. *Maryland Gazette*, Sept. 7, 1752.

51. Schultz, *History of Freemasonry in Maryland* 1:28.

52. Irving Lowens, *A Bibliography of Songsters Printed in America before 1821* (Worcester: American Antiquarian Society, 1976), p. 3.

53. Lawrence C. Wroth, *A History of Printing in Colonial Maryland* (Baltimore: Typothetae, 1922), pp. 82–83; *Maryland Gazette*, Jan. 17, 1754; Hamilton, "History" 3:299.

54. Lowens, *A Bibliography of Songsters*, p. 3.

55. *Maryland Gazette*, Sept. 19, 1754; possibly by John Bacon, an officer of the company and son of the Reverend Thomas Bacon.

56. Hamilton, "History" 3:548–50. This portion is located in the Dulany Papers, MS. 1265, Maryland Historical Society, Baltimore; Breslaw, ed., *Records*, sederunt 237, Feb. 25, 1755.

57. Hamilton, "History" 1:162, 339.

58. Caleb Dorsey account book, D. S. Ridgely Papers (1733–1884), MS. 717, Maryland Historical Society, Baltimore. Dorsey's account book includes transactions with Charles Cole. Leveridge's original setting, titled "The Cobler's End," is found in *The Musical Miscellany* (London: Watts, 1729), 2:170–71; and in Bickham's *Musical Entertainer* ([London]: C. Corbett, [1737]), 1:36.

59. Henry Callister, letter to William Tear, Nov. 5, 1745, Callister Papers.

60. Hamilton, "History" 3:505, MS. 1265, Maryland Historical Society; Breslaw, ed., *Records*, sederunt 233, Dec. 16, 1754.

61. Henry Callister, letter to William Tear, Nov. 5, 1745, Callister Papers.

62. Hamilton, "History" 3:136; Breslaw, ed., *Records*, sederunt 188, Oct. 26, 1752.

63. Hamilton, "History" 1:57. Hamilton listed Italian composers and singers familiar to British audiences; among the more obscure musicians were composer Carlo Tessarini (b. 1690) and Valentini, who may have been either Giuseppi Valentini (b. 1681), a

composer whose works were published in London, or Valentino Urbani Valentini (fl. London, 1707–15), who appeared in Bononcini's *Almahide*, performed in London in 1711. Singers included Benedetti (fl. London, 1720–22), who appeared in another Bononcini opera, *Crispo*, performed in London in 1722, and the rival castrati Farinelli and Senesino. Auretti, Violante, and Berberini are not to be found in principal reference works but were probably popular opera singers of the day.

64. Henry Callister, letter to William Tear, Nov. 5, 1745, Callister Papers.

65. John W. Molnar, "A Collection of Music in Colonial Virginia: The Ogle Inventory," *Musical Quarterly* 49 (1963): 150–62; and Maurer, "The Library of a Colonial Musician," pp. 39–52.

66. Lemay, *Men of Letters*, p. 322.

67. Maurer, "The Library of a Colonial Musician," pp. 39–52; Molnar, "A Collection of Music in Colonial Virginia," pp. 150–62. Ogle was, for a short time, a London impresario. Molnar's speculations concerning repertoire not specifically identified in the inventory were based on Ogle's concert notices in the *London Daily Advertiser*, 1751–52.

68. W. H. Grattan Flood, "Eighteenth Century Italians in Dublin," *Music & Letters* 3 (1922): 274–78.

69. Henry Callister, letter to William Tear, Nov. 5, 1745, Callister Papers.

70. Robert J. Micklus, "Dr. Alexander Hamilton's 'The History of the Tuesday Club'" (Ph.D. diss., University of Delaware, 1980), 1:xiii.

71. *The Principles of Practicle Musick . . . Either in Singing or Playing upon an Instrument* (London: W. Godbid for Henry Brome, 1665). "An enlarged edition (1667) was described as a compendium of 'Practicall Musick in five parts teaching by a new and easie method. 1. The rudiments of Song. 2. The principles of composition. 3. The use of discords. 4. The form of Figurate Discant. 5. The contrivance of Canon'"; see E. Herron-Allen and Robert Donington, "Simpson, Christopher," *Grove's Dictionary of Music and Musicians*, 5th ed., 7:798. Malcolm's *Treatise of Musick, Speculative, Practical and Historical* (Edinburgh: n.p., 1721) also came out in a second edition of 1731 (London) and a third edition (1751) and was mentioned in the *Gentleman's Magazine* for Aug. 1751. Revised editions were published in London in 1776 and 1779 under the title *Malcolm's Treatise of Music Corrected and Abridged by an Eminent Musician;* see James R. Heintze, "Alexander Malcolm: Musician, Clergyman, and Schoolmaster," *Maryland Historical Magazine* 73 (1978): 233n. William Tans'ur's *New Musical Grammar* (London, 1746) was eventually published in 1772 as *The Elements of Musick Display'd;* see Nicholas Temperley, "Tans'ur, William," *The New Grove Dictionary of Music and Musicians*, ed. Stanley Sadie (London: Macmillan, 1980), 18:567.

72. Thomas Bacon, letter to Henry Callister, Jan. 28, 1746, Callister Papers.

73. Malcolm's *Treatise* is cited in John C. Pepusch, *A Treatise on Harmony* (London: Pearson, 1731); Johann Walther, *Musikalisches Lexikon* (Leipzig: Deer, 1732); James Grassineau, *A Musical Dictionary, Being a Collection of Terms and Characters* (London: Wilcox, 1740); Jacob Adlung, *Anleitung zu der musikalischen Gelahrtheit* (Erfurt: Jungnicol, 1758); and others. See Heintze, "Alexander Malcolm," p. 234n.

74. J. A. Fuller-Maitland, *The Oxford History of Music*, vol. 4, *The Age of Bach & Handel* (Oxford: Clarendon, 1902), p. 346.

75. For an analysis of Malcolm's *Treatise*, see Reppard Stone, "An Evaluative Study of Alexander Malcolm's 'Treatise of Music: Speculative, Practical and Historical'" (Ph.D. diss., Catholic University, 1974).

76. Marcus A. McCorison, ed., *The 1764 Catalog of the Redwood Library Company at Newport, Rhode Island* (New Haven: Yale University Press, 1965), p. 54.

77. Philip Vickers Fithian, *Journal & Letters of Philip Vickers Fithian, 1773–1774: A Plantation Tutor of the Old Dominion*, ed. Hunter Dickinson Farish (Williamsburg, Va.: Colonial Williamsburg, 1943), p. 288.

78. Henry Callister, letter to Dr. Troup, Apr. 2, 1765, Callister Papers.

79. Henry Callister, letter to Anthony Bacon, Oct. 21, 1747, Callister Papers.

80. Hamilton, "History" 2:359; Breslaw, ed., *Records*, sederunt 155, May 14, 1751.

81. Breslaw, ed., *Records*, sederunt 165, Oct. 8, 1751.

82. *Maryland Gazette*, Oct. 12, 1752.

83. Ibid., June 14, 1753.

84. Lemay, *Men of Letters*, p. 322.

85. Hamilton, "History" 2:392, describes a special Thursday meeting that followed the anniversary of May 14, 1751. His drawing of this event (p. 397) reveals a French horn, drum, and violin. Bacon, Malcolm, Hamilton, Wolstenholme, and Daniel Dulany, Jr., were present; the last-named may have been the third violinist depicted on p. 358 in Hamilton's sketch of a rehearsal of May 24, 1751. The ensemble for the Thursday meeting itself (May 16, 1751) probably consisted of three violins, flute, cello, horn, and drum. See Breslaw, ed., *Records*, sederunt 156, May 16, 1751.

86. For example, Breslaw, ed., *Records*, sederunt 157, May 28, 1751: "Sir John Sung the first chorus to the ode most manfully, being accompanied by a fiddle Solo." Ibid., sederunt 195, Feb. 6, 1753; and Hamilton, "History" 3:153, record that the "Grand Chorus for the year 1751" was performed by Hamilton (cello), Malcolm (violin), and William Lux (organ).

87. Breslaw, ed., *Records*, sederunt 101, Mar. 14, 1749; sederunt 139, Sept. 18, 1750; and sederunt 169, Dec. 10, 1751.

88. Henry Callister, letter to William Tear, Nov. 5, 1745, Callister Papers.

89. *Maryland Gazette*, Nov. 28, 1750; Schultz, *History of Freemasonry in Maryland* 1:30–31.

4

MUSIC AND THE TUESDAY CLUB

Introduction

The Tuesday Club encouraged intellectual and artistic activity of a re-
markably high level by bringing together some of the brightest, best-
educated, and most creative Marylanders. Men of ability rather than of
high station were invited into the club. Although no specific require-
ments for membership appear in contemporaneous writings, it is obvious
from the diversity of national, social, and professional backgrounds that
wit, intellectual curiosity, and a love of music were qualities highly valued
in the Tuesday Club.

Alexander Hamilton founded this organization in May 1745[1] and
served as its secretary from July of that year, inspiring and sustaining his
beloved club until shortly before his death in May 1756.[2] Hamilton clearly
provided the energy and imagination that made the club possible; following his death the club disbanded.[3]

The Tuesday Club met on alternate Tuesdays, usually at the homes
of members. Most sederunts were attended by six to twelve members
and guests. Evening activities usually began with dinner, followed by a
prescribed series of toasts, some of which were sung. The after-dinner
period was devoted to matters concerning the regulation of the club, official business, and various other endeavors that reveal a remarkable range
of interests and creative abilities.

In addition to their music, the members composed poetry; the health
and well-being of the club's president was a favorite topic—specifically,
Cole's periodically incapacitating gout. A sample from "Carmen Secu-
lare" follows:

> Ah wretched Club! must thou again,
> Resume the lamentable Strain
> By cruel fates doom'd once a year
> To Sigh, and shed the doleful tear.[4]

"Lugubris Cantus," similarly inspired, appeared on the front page of the *Maryland Gazette* for January 16, 1751. The poet laureate, Jonas Green, contributed several extended works, including anniversary odes and a "Heroic Poem" that exceeds 500 lines;[5] other poems were penned by individual members such as William Lux, who produced "Ah, What's Become of Noble Jole at This Unlucky Time."[6]

Various word games delighted the members; among these were acrostics, coded puzzles, and conundrums. Commencing with the meeting of January 30, 1750, Hamilton and Green were each required to produce two conundrums (riddles whose answers involve a pun) for every meeting. If the club solved the riddles, the author toasted the club with a "bumper"; if the members failed to guess the correct answer, the author was declared "victor." In the latter case, the members were required to toast the author.[7] The following conundrums are typical:

> Query: Why is a pewter plate like a Certain Seminary of Learning?
> Answer: Because it is Eat-on.[8]
>
> Query: Why is a dancing master like a Shade tree?
> Answer: Because he is full of bows—boughs.[9]

These conundrums were often gently bawdy. They became controversial because some of the members were not sufficiently clever to solve the riddles; conundrums were consequently banned after September 18, 1750.[10]

The club issued formal letters and commissions, and members presented addresses and philosophical discourses. A branch of the club, established in Talbot County, Maryland, and called the Eastern Shore Triumvirate, was essentially a musical society, composed of merchant Robert Morris and the Reverends John Gordon and Thomas Bacon.[11] The governance of the club was a primary concern; its members enacted no less than fifty laws concerning all aspects of club life—the powers of the president, the disposition of its charity fund, permissible menus, and circumstances requiring members to laugh or sing were but a few of the areas regulated by club legislation. Many Tuesday Club members participated in the colonial government; the legal debates of the club often satirized the more serious debates of the colonial legislature.[12]

The casual conversation of the club, although unrecorded, must have been stimulating, considering the character of its members and visitors. Prominent scientists, artists, politicians, musicians, theologians, and members of America's wealthiest families appear in the records. Benjamin Franklin, Dr. Adam Thomson, painters Hesselius and Wollaston, Benjamin Tasker, Charles Carroll, Benedict Calvert, Charles Love, Edward

Lloyd, and the Bordley, Dulany, and Holliday families were attracted to the club, whose activities were succinctly described in an anniversary speech of June 16, 1752: "We meet, converse, Laugh, talk Smoke, drink, differ, agree, Philosophize, Harangue, pun, Sing, Dance and fiddle together."[13]

Club Composers

The principal composers of the club were Alexander Hamilton, Thomas Bacon, and probably Alexander Malcolm. They performed more frequently than other musical members and guests, and the 1750 and 1751 anniversary odes are attributed to Hamilton and Bacon, respectively, in the club's history.[14] The third extant ode, composed "by several hands," appears with this commentary:

> Then the music of the anniversary ode was plaid over, not composed, as may be plainly seen, by Signior Lardini [Bacon] but collected from the works of several celebrated composers. The Chancellor [Malcolm] performed the violino primo, Squeak Grumbleton, Esq. [John Wollaston], a stranger invited to the Club did the violino secondo, and the Secretary [Hamilton], the violoncello while Mr. Protomusicus and Crinkum Crankum Esqrs. [Thornton and Lux] managed the vocal part.[15]

The phrase "collected from the works of celebrated composers" suggests a compilation of existing music, a common practice of the period, often mistakenly attributed as original composition. However, the music of the 1753 ode is of an uneven, amateurish quality, containing such technical errors and inconsistencies as to make extensive borrowing from established eighteenth-century composers unlikely. Hamilton's history points out that Bacon was not the composer. William Lux, the club's clavier performer, may have possessed sufficient skill to compose music. Lux did perform the vocal part, and he also may well have assisted in its composition; but the compositional errors in the 1753 ode are not typical of a keyboard composer, who would have discovered obvious dissonances by playing all parts of the ode simultaneously, a practice not possible for a string player.

William Thornton might also have been among the contributors; he is named as composer of a "club jigg."[16] Charles Cole, president, was also known to improvise melodies.[17] Hamilton probably wrote the solo violoncello passage in the overture to the 1753 ode and possibly collaborated with Malcolm, who remains the most likely principal composer of the 1753 ode. Although James Heintze has written that Malcolm was not a composer, Malcolm's treatise attests to his familiarity with rules of eighteenth-

century counterpoint, and his performance as first violinist in the ode
suggests a central role in its composition.[18] Of the potential composers'
musical training, virtually nothing has come to light.

Alexander Hamilton (1712–56) was born in Edinburgh, where his
father was principal of the university.[19] He had several brothers, most notably Dr. John Hamilton, who immigrated to the colonies before him, and
Gavin Hamilton, a bookseller and publisher with whom Alexander corre-
sponded after arriving in Maryland.[20] Alexander Hamilton received his
M.D. degree from the University of Edinburgh in 1737 and, following
additional study in pharmacy, relocated in Annapolis in 1739.[21] Tuesday
Club friendships may have led to his marriage to Margaret Dulany in
1747, bringing Hamilton into one of the colony's wealthiest and most
prominent families; three of Margaret's brothers were either members or
frequent guests of the club.[22] Hamilton was intensely active in the community, serving as a vestryman of St. Anne's Church, representing Annapolis in the Maryland legislature, and promoting various works in the
public interest, such as the Talbot County Free School and improvements
in the city dock.[23]

Hamilton was also a writer of considerable importance to the modern reader. His most important literary works include *Itinerarium*, an account of an extended journey through the mid-Atlantic and New England colonies undertaken in 1744, and his voluminous Tuesday Club
manuscripts. The *Itinerarium* is a most valuable commentary on colonial
society, containing much detailed information about city and country life.
Hamilton recorded not only what he saw but also what he heard from
residents and fellow travelers and even added his own critical observations.[24] This commentary is invaluable when comparing the cultural activity of Annapolis with that of northern cities. As a gentleman and a
member of the aristocracy, Hamilton enjoyed access to all levels of society.
His observations substantiate the claim that Annapolis, although small,
could boast a society of considerable sophistication. It is indeed noteworthy that Hamilton, upon arrival from Annapolis, found Philadelphia
somewhat dull:

> I never was in a place so populous where the *gout* for publick gay
> diversions prevailed so little. There is no such thing as assem-
> blies of the gentry among them, either for dancing or musick;
> these they have had an utter aversion to ever since Whitefield
> preached among them. . . . Some Virginia gentlemen that came
> here with the Commissioners of the Indian treaty were desirous
> of having a ball, but could find none of the female sex in a hu-
> mor for it.[25]

Philadelphia was not entirely without music. On his return through
that city, Hamilton was guest at a "Musick Club":

I paid a visit to Collector Alexander in the afternoon, and at night going to the coffee-house, I went from thence, along with Messrs. Wallace and Currie, to the Musick Club, where I heard a tolerable *concerto* performed by a harpsichord and three violins. One Levy there played a very good violin; one Quin bore another pretty good part; Tench Francis played a very indifferent finger upon an excellent violin that once belonged to the late Ch. Calvert, Governour of Maryland. We dismissed ourselves with musick, and good viands and liquor.[26]

Hamilton, however, had a higher opinion of Boston's cultural life: "Assemblies of the gayer sort are frequent here, the gentlemen and ladies meeting almost every week at concerts of musick and balls. I was present at two or three such, and saw as fine a ring of ladies, as good dancing, and heard musick as elegant as I had been witness to anywhere."[27] He encountered another Bostonian in a New York club:

But the most remarkable person in the whole company was one Wendall, a young gentleman from Boston. He entertained us mightily by playing on the violin the quickest tunes upon the highest keys, which he accompanied with his voice, so as even to drown out the violin, with such nice shakings and gracings that I thought his voice out did the instrument. . . . The like I never heard, and the thing seemed to me next a miracle. The extent of his voice is impossible to describe even to imagine unless by hearing him. The whole company was amazed that any person but a woman or eunuch could have such a pipe, and began to question his virility; but he swore that if the company pleased he would show a couple of as good witnesses as any man might wear.

The performer then imitated the sounds of barnyard animals to great acclaim.[28]

It is apparent from his account that taverns and clubs provided the primary public outlet for serious music in colonial cities. Clubs frequently met in taverns, and their musical activities were consequently quite public: "At night I went to a tavern fronting the Albany coffee-house along with Doctor Colchoun where I heard a *concerto* of musick, performed by one violin and two German flutes. The violin was by far the best I had heard played since I came to America. It was handled by one Mr. H——d."[29]

Homes provided another opportunity for music making but sometimes presented special problems, as illustrated by the following description of a private performance in Boston:

I went to change at twelve o'clock and dined with Mr. Arbuthnot. I had a tune on the spinet from his daughter after dinner who is a pretty, agreeable lady, and sings well. I told her that she played the best spinet that I had heard since I came to America. The old man, who is a blunt, honest fellow, asked me if I could pay her no other compliment but that, which dashed me a little; but I soon replied that the young lady was in every way so deserving and accomplished that nothing that was spoke in her commendation could in a strict sense be called a compliment. I breathed a little after this speech, there being something romantic in it, and considering human nature in a proper light, the old man was pleased and picked his teeth; and I was conscious that I had talked nonsense.[30]

One of the many people whom Hamilton met during his travels was to become a lifelong friend. Describing his first encounter, in Marblehead, with Alexander Malcolm, who subsequently moved to Annapolis, Hamilton wrote:

I put up here at one Reid's at the sign of the Dragon, and while I was at dinner, Mr. Malcolm, the Church of England minister to whom I was recommended, came in. After I had dined he carried me round the town. . . . I went to his house and drank tea with him. He showed me some pretty pieces of music, and played some tunes on the flute and violin. He is author of a very good book upon music, which shows his judgement and knowledge in that part of science.[31]

During his journey Hamilton attended many religious services. He seldom made mention of sacred music, but in a Roman Catholic mass in Philadelphia, he "heard some musick" at the "Roman Chapel," but added that the "indegestible" reasonings of the priest made him ill.[32] Of a synagogue in New York he mentioned "lugubrious songs."[33] In Boston he attended "English chapel" with a Mr. Lechmere and heard a "small organ played by an indifferent organist."[34]

Hamilton's only account of music accompanying a public event is his description of the proclamation of war against France, given at Philadelphia on June 11, 1744:

There were about two hundred gentlemen attended Governour [George] Thomas. Col. [Thomas] Lee, of Virginia, walked at his right hand, and Secretary [Richard] Peters upon his left; the procession was led by about thirty flags and ensigns taken from privateer vessels and others in the harbour, which were carried by a parcel of roaring sailors. They were followed by eight or ten drums that made a confounded martial noise but all the instrumental music they had was a pitiful scraping negro fiddle, which followed the drums and could not be heard for the noise and clamor of the people and the rattle of the drums. There was a rabble of about 4,000 people in the street, and great numbers of ladies and gentlemen in the windows and balconies.[35]

Negro fiddlers were common in the colonies. Hamilton's casual reference to another such fiddler heard on board a sloop near Albany, New York, suggests nothing extraordinary. Furthermore, both the *Virginia Gazette* and the *Maryland Gazette* (see p. 24) carried notices of runaway slaves who could have been identified by their musical prowess as violinists.[36]

Although his *Itinerarium* is laced with humor, it is in Hamilton's letters and essays, some of which were published in the *Maryland Gazette*, and in his Tuesday Club manuscripts that his satirical gifts were put to full use. Among Hamilton's contributions to the *Gazette* was a satire on "The Baltimore Belles"[37] (a poem written by Thomas Chase and Thomas Cradock), numerous letters, and a sprightly, thoroughly enjoyable essay on the commonplace colonial greeting "What's News?" published in the *Maryland Gazette* of January 7, 1746.[38] This essay was a literary history and critique of the *Gazette* for the first year of Green's ownership.

Hamilton's masterpiece is the "History of the Ancient and Honorable Tuesday Club," begun in 1754. Consisting of twelve books, it is a fanciful account of the club's activities interspersed with essays on a variety of subjects. In "Of History and Historians," the first chapter of book 1, Hamilton points out that "the transactions of Empires, Kingdoms, Republics and Clubs yield an Inexhaustible fund of matter."[39] In the succeeding chapters, "Of Antiquity, Its Dignity and Importance," "Of Clubs in General, and Their Antiquity," and "Some Scraps of Ancient History Relating to Clubs,"[40] Hamilton points out that clubs are as worthy a subject for historical study as any other topic and proceeds to trace their development from antediluvian origins through Noah in extraordinarily meandering prose.

> Immediately after the Deluge, we find Noe given to Clubbing, for he plants a vinyard and drinks the juice of the grape with his bon-companions, and gets fuddled, and this, for aught we can find from scraps and fragments of ancient History, was the first origin of Fuddling Clubs, and it is said, that some members drank so hard, at the first Institution of these fuddle-cap societies, that their countenances turned florid, then purple, and at last they plied so hard, that many became black in the face with mere force of drinking, and this, I think, more naturally accounts for the origin of the Moors and Negroes, than any other fine spun reasons that have been delivered to the Accademie Royal de Sciences, or any other learned society on earth, who have proffered very great Rewards to the literati, to account reasonably for this strange phenomenon, and, as I look

upon myself, to be the author of this very useful Discovery, I hope the Republic of letters will allot me a handsome reward suitable to my merit, at least I expect a medal from the Royal Society, and to be entered a member of that learned body, as the smallest recompense for my study and application in making this important discovery; I may meet with some, perhaps, who may treat me, as his contemporary Physicians treated Doctor Harvey, when he first discovered the circulation of the blood, who maintained that Hippocrates, Galen and many others were the first discoverers of it.[41]

The length of this single sentence is characteristic of the writer's unique style.

Although the content may appear mannered and frivolous, Hamilton claimed that both his satire and his club bore a closer resemblance to real life than other accounts and activities that were thought to be more serious. In his preface he states:

Some people, who may find time enough to throw away in the reading of this, will undoubtedly exclaim, well! and what the deuce is the meaning of these grave observations? I'll tell them in short what they mean; many, I am satisfied, will either be mightily astonished, or pretend to be so, that any mortal wight, could waste, as they call it, so much precious time, besides paper and ink in compiling and collecting the History of (as it may seem to them) a Ridiculous Club, whose chief pastime (they'll say) appears from the face of the History itself, and from the Grotesque Stile of its idle author, to have been the carrying on, a silly, stupid, and unmeaning farce. Very well, my good friends, what if I should grant you all this, since you are pleased to assert it, the subject of this History is a farce and a very silly one too, since you will needs have it so, I will not indeed so easily grant you that it is an unmeaning one, since it bears an exact resemblance to many other farces of human life, esteemed (tho' they are not really so) of a more serious nature.[42]

Hamilton's accounts of the club's activities given in his history appear to be factual, inasmuch as they agree with his records, which we suppose to be accurate. The satire is confined to the significance of those activities and to the identification of the members.

Hamilton cannot be considered an influential writer. His major works were not published during his lifetime; indeed, the *Itinerarium* was not printed until 1907, and his history is still to be read only in manuscript or typescript copy.[43] His writing, like his music, was intended for his own amusement and for the private entertainment of his friends. His literary legacy—*Itinerarium* and the Tuesday Club documents—reveals him as an acute observer, a social critic, and one of America's first and finest humorists. Physician, legislator, churchman, author, performer, and composer, Hamilton was truly a Renaissance man, and the Tuesday Club was a perfect medium for his many interests. In February 1756 Hamilton's failing health prompted him to relinquish his post of secretary. In a touching farewell letter, filled with typical wit and grace, he entrusted the club's records to William Lux:

> February 11th 1756
>
> Sir
>
> I am sorry I cannot attend the Club this Night, which is a great Disappointment to myself, as I always take great Pleasure in the Club. However as his Honor will not be present with you to Night (which I know by his sending to me for a Vial of Sal Volatile) my Presence will be the less necessary, so the Attorney General cannot go on with the Trial against me, unless he prosecutes *Coram non [?] Justice*, which (in my Opinion) would be a Practice Clubically extrajudicial.
>
> I have sent you herewith the Records, of which you are to take 'special care, let them be well kept, and produced at next Sederunt, when (as I take it) Dr. Upton Scott serves the Club. For the loss of these Archives (in my Opinion), would be greater to Posterity than the Loss of the whole Transactions of Alexander the Great; for I think Charles Cole the great to be a greater Man than the former, in so far as he has done less Harm to Mankind; the Office of the first being that of a Cutthroat, and the Occupation of the other the keeping of a Store in a reputable and Merchant-like Manner, in North East Street in Annapolis, and (the most glorious of all his Occupations) the Ruling of the ancient and honorable Tuesday Club these ten years past, with Justice, Equity and Moderation. I doubt [not?] his Honour is ill with the Gout, therefore it will be proper for the Poet Laureat, or the Club to compose dolorous Versiculi on that Occasion, to be properly presented.
>
> I am Sir your most humble Servt.
> Alexr. Hamilton Secretary[44]

On Tuesday, May 11, 1756, the eleventh anniversary of the founding of the club, Hamilton died. Jonas Green published his obituary in the *Maryland Gazette* of the following Thursday:

> On Tuesday last in the Morning, Died, at his House in this City, Alexander Hamilton, M.D. Aged 44 Years. The Death of this valuable and worthy Gentleman is universally and justly la-

mented: His medical Abilities, various Knowledge, strictness of Integrity, simplicity of Manners, and extensive Benevolence, having deservedly gained him the Respect and Esteem of all Ranks of Men.—No man, in his Sphere, has left fewer Enemies, or more Friends.[45]

Many years later Dr. Upton Scott received the Tuesday Club histories from Hamilton's widow and, in 1809, loaned them to the Library Company of Baltimore. In an accompanying letter, Scott wrote of the club's demise:

> He founded the Tuesday Club, of which he might be considered the life and soul, as it expired with him, having never assembled after his death. . . . I was early invited as a visitor to the Tuesday Club, and soon afterwards elected a *Long Standing* member thereof, and am now, I believe, the only survivor of that Institution, at whose merry meetings I often in my younger days found much amusement. Many years after Dr. Hamilton's death, I received this work as a present from his widow, who was a lady highly worthy of my esteem and regard. I cannot therefore obtain my own consent to part with in my lifetime,—the property, of what I consider as a sacred relick, or memorial of deceased friends.[46]

The most accomplished club composer, Thomas Bacon (1700?–1768), was born on the Isle of Man, according to most histories; recent scholarship, however, indicates that he was a native of Whitehaven, Cumberland County, England.[47] The earliest known record of his existence places him in charge of a coal depot in Dublin sometime before 1737, the year in which he published his "Book of Rates," entitled *A Compleat System of the Revenue of Ireland.*[48] With his first marriage Bacon acquired a second business, a coffeehouse, and there established yet another enterprise in January 1742, with the publication of his newspaper the *Dublin Mercury,* "Printed by Thomas Bacon, Printer and Bookseller, at Bacon's Coffee-House in Essex-Street." In September of that same year, he received permission to print the official newspaper of Ireland, the *Dublin Gazette.*[49] As a publisher and bookseller, Bacon gained access to the literary world. He journeyed to London, where he met Thomas Osbourne, the famous London bookseller. Osbourne introduced him to Samuel Richardson, who negotiated with Bacon for the marketing of his highly successful novel *Pamela.*[50] An avid amateur musician and newspaper publisher, Bacon must have been exposed to Dublin's musical life. The year 1742 also came to be highly significant in the annals of music history; on April 10 Bacon's *Mercury* announced "The Messiah, Mr. Handell's Sacred Oratorio, which in the Opinion of the best judges, far surpasses anything of that Nature, which has been performed in this or any other Kingdom."[51] The following week the performance was reviewed: "Words are wanting to express the most exquisite Delight it afforded to the admiring crowded Audiences. The sublime, the grand, and the tender, adapted to the most elevated, majestic, and moving Words."[52]

At the advanced age of forty-three, Bacon again determined to enter a new profession. He ceased publishing the *Gazette* in July 1743 and undertook preparation for the ministry, studying with Bishop Wilson, on the Isle of Man.[53] He immigrated to Maryland in 1745, accompanied by his wife and son, and took up residence in Talbot County, where he served as curate of St. Peter's Parish.[54] His reasons for choosing Maryland are unknown, but he was probably encouraged by the success of his brother Anthony Bacon, who had made his fortune in Maryland, returned to England in 1740, and later entered Parliament.[55] Although Thomas Bacon never resided in Annapolis, both his performances with the Tuesday Club and his membership in its Eastern Shore branch (the Triumvirate) justify his designation as one of the capital's leading musicians.

Like Hamilton, Bacon was a prolific writer, but, unlike his learned friend, Bacon actually had much of his own work published. He did, in fact, publish more titles than any other colonial Marylander. His literary output was serious and also remarkable in its diversity. By the time of his death, he was moderately well known, having published in Ireland, England, and America. Many of his sermons were printed in London by John Oliver and in America by Jonas Green, who also published Bacon's monumental compilation of the *Laws of Maryland* in 1765.[56]

Over the years Bacon emerged as the colony's leading clergyman. An enlightened minister and educator, he promoted free schools in Talbot and Frederick counties and was among the first American clergymen to advocate education for slaves. In his sermons he further assured the slaves that they could have as great a share of heaven as their masters, an advanced idea in an age that witnessed theological debates on whether or not slaves possessed souls.[57] When Maryland's Anglican clergy met in 1753 to determine their best course of action for curtailing the growth of Catholicism and dissenting Protestant sects such as the Presbyterians, one faction argued for governmental suppression of the encroaching faiths, but Bacon, sensitive to the colonists' resentment of the established church, led a moderate and more tolerant faction whose opinion prevailed. Thereafter, Bacon was widely recognized as an unofficial spokesman for the clergy of Maryland's established church.[58]

Bacon practiced what he preached, promoting and raising funds for a charity school in Talbot County, a project supported by his Tuesday Club friends, most notably Hamilton and Green.[59] He employed his considerable musical skills to the same purpose, preaching and performing benefit concerts in Williamsburg and Upper Marlborough, enlisting the aid of club musicians and the visiting theatrical company for benefit performances in Annapolis. Bacon even succeeded in obtaining the support of the governor of Virginia and Lord Baltimore.[60] The school was completed in 1755, but the death of a major benefactor and a period of economic hardship resulted in diminished financial support; the school closed sometime before 1760.[61]

The mid-1750s were difficult years for Bacon. His wife died in 1755, and his only son was killed in the French and Indian War.[62] He was indicted for rape but successfully sued his accuser for libel.[63] Bacon remarried in 1757 but was fined 5,000 pounds of tobacco for failing to publish the marriage banns.[64] He experienced financial difficulties, and his music suffered; in October 1757 he wrote: "A man without money or credit must do as he can. . . . Musick is departed and gone into another world for me. The Laws are my only employment & Amusement; yet they are a dry sort of Stuff and sometimes apt to stick in the throat."[65] Bacon's financial situation improved dramatically in 1758, when he became rector of All Saints Parish, Frederick, Maryland, the most lucrative pulpit in the colony.[66] He remained in Frederick until his death in 1768.

Bacon's playing of the violin and viola da gamba have already been noted; he may also have been proficient on the harpsichord.[67] As a composer he was probably self-taught, relying on such treatises as Christopher Simpson's *Compendium*, which he recommended to Callister (see p. 35). His compositions display the influence of the Italian musicians who were prominently featured in Dublin's concert life,[68] and Bacon may have had some contact with Dublin's Italian music school. His club pseudonym, "Signior Lardini," certainly indicates that he was regarded by his friends as a composer in the Italian tradition. We have at least one significant clue to Bacon's involvement as a Dublin musician; one of his compositions, a catch, entitled "See, See, My Boys," was published in a Dublin collection of catches dedicated to the Hibernian Catch Club.[69] This appearance of Bacon's composition, the approximate date of publication (1786), and the attribution to "Rev. Mr. Bacon" suggest that Bacon had been a member of this musical club while in Dublin, that he remained in contact with members of Dublin's musical life after his move to the colonies, and that his compositions were popular on both sides of the Atlantic for a considerable period after his death. Bacon's Maryland popularity is substantiated by the appearance of one of his minuets in the collection of John Ormsby (see p. 31) and by the observation of a contemporary biographer, Jonathan Boucher.[70] Bacon was a "modern" composer, writing in a simple *style galant* of more than a little elegance and grace. His "Minuet for the Attorney General," composed "on the spot," is indicative of his facility.[71]

In the year of his death, 1768, Bacon was elected a member of the American Philosophical Society, the oldest learned society in America, founded in Philadelphia by Benjamin Franklin in 1743.[72] Such was Bacon's prominence in the American colonies that his obituary appeared in Maryland, Virginia, and Pennsylvania newspapers.[73]

The only Tuesday Club musician known to the international musical community, Alexander Malcolm (1685–1763), arrived in Annapolis rather late in life and, following a visit in 1748, was appointed rector of St. Anne's Church in 1749. Before immigrating to America about 1732, he had been employed as a schoolmaster in Aberdeen and Edinburgh and had published three major works on bookkeeping and arithmetic in addition to his renowned treatise on music. He came to the colonies as a teacher and served as master of a grammar school in the city of New York between 1732 and 1740. In the latter year, at the age of fifty-five, Malcolm was granted missionary status by the Society for the Propagation of the Gospel in Foreign Parts and, like Bacon, became a clergyman late in life.

His first parish was the church at Marblehead, Massachusetts, where his enlightened sermons were enjoyed by dissenters as well as by his own parishioners.[74] In 1744 he was visited by Alexander Hamilton, who recounted the visit in his *Itinerarium:* "I went to his house and had tea with him. He showed me some pretty pieces of music, and played some tunes on the flute and violin. He is author of a very good book upon music, which shows his judgment and knowledge in that part of science." The following day, Sunday, July 29, Hamilton attended Malcolm's church twice, a most unusual event, and commented that Malcolm "gave us a pretty discourse."[75] This was high praise considering that, throughout his *Itinerarium*, Hamilton was critical of preachers, and his literary output in general evidences his suspicions about the intellectual depth of most clergymen. Although little that transpired between the two has been recorded, it is certain that Malcolm had found in Hamilton a kindred spirit: for the better part of three days, Malcolm escorted the Annapolitan through the surrounding countryside and introduced him to prominent citizens of the area.[76] Hamilton's visit was likely a factor in Malcolm's decision to relocate in Maryland. Never one to balk at change, Malcolm decided to take on both a new parish and a new wife in 1748, at the remarkable age of sixty-three.[77] He became a member of the Tuesday Club and was soon appointed its chancellor. This grand old man appears as a colorful figure in the club records, which often reveal aspects of his character not commonly associated with the clergy.

For the colonial musician, Malcolm's *Treatise of Musick, Speculative, Practical and Historical* (1721) may have been particularly helpful, in light of the relative scarcity of competent instruction in music theory and composition. In addition to chapters on the history and philosophy of music, the work includes fundamentals—notation, rhythm, meter, transposition, clefs, and intervals—as well as simple instruction in such compositional elements as melody, harmony, modulation, and counterpoint, illustrated with musical examples. Physical aspects of sound, including intervallic ratios, are also considered.

Although Malcolm described equal temperament, he was a proponent of just intonation and, as a practical matter, added directions for tuning a harpsichord. Despite its advocacy of just temperament, the *Treatise* is very much a forward-looking work. Firmly committed to the major-minor system of tonality, Malcolm anticipated the simpler forms of counterpoint found in Johann Fux's *Gradus ad Parnassum* (1725) and revealed concepts of harmony that were extended by Jean-Philippe Rameau in his *Traité de l'harmonie* (1722).[78]

It is peculiar that Malcolm's musical reputation was given so little notice in Tuesday Club documents; possibly he did not want to compete in any way with the club's designated musicians. In any event it is hard to believe that one who had made such a thorough study of music theory did not exert a shaping force on the club's musical compositions, especially on those pieces ostensibly written by "several hands."

Malcolm found the duties of St. Anne's Church too strenuous because of his age, and in 1753 he requested a transfer to a less demanding parish. Governor Sharpe granted the request and assigned Malcolm to St. Paul's in Queen Anne's County.[79] Malcolm's final appearance at the Tuesday Club was on June 11, 1754.[80] After moving across the Chesapeake, he continued an active schedule of parish duties, serving also as schoolmaster for the Queen Anne's County Free School.[81] He died on June 15, 1763.[82] His obituary in the *Maryland Gazette* reads: "A few days ago Died, in an advanced Age, in Queen-Anne's County, The Reverend ALEXANDER MALCOLM, A.M. Rector of St. Paul's Parish in that County: A Gentleman who has obliged the World with several learned Performances on the Mathematics, Music, and Grammar."[83]

Other Club Composers

William Thornton (d. 1769), sheriff of Anne Arundel County, was also a merchant and shipowner. His sloop probably was used in the West Indian trade, since his advertisements in the *Maryland Gazette* featured rum, sugar, and oranges.[84]

Thornton was the official club musician, known as Protomusicus Solo Neverout.[85] He possessed such a superior voice that he was required to sing his votes in the club; otherwise, they would not be counted: "William Thornton, Esqr., on account of his uncommon talent in Singing was by unanimous consent of the Club appointed Proto-musicus or chief musician con voce of the Club and it is ordained, that as often as he votes in Club, he is to Sing his vote in a musical manner."[86] Furthermore, Thornton was not allowed to play musical instruments. This may have been a facetious prohibition since there is no record of his ever having successfully performed on one;[87] on the other hand, the "Grand Club Jig by Signior Protomusicus," strongly suggests some instrumental ability.[88]

Thornton improvised tunes for some of the club's songs such as Green's anniversary ode for the year 1749: "When the poet had read this Ode, the Club approved of it, and the Chorus only was Sung by Mr. Musician Thornton, who by the asistance of Mr. Samuel Hart, an honorary member, a gentleman remarkable for his delicate pipe, Set a tune to it, the performance of the Rest being deferred, till the Club procures their band of Instrumental music."[89] This may have been an original melody, but, more likely, Thornton simply adapted an existing tune to Green's text. Such a procedure, typical of the eighteenth century, is evident in another club song for which Thornton sang "a Recitative and excellent old tune to a great part of the poet Laureat's heroic Poem."[90]

Charles Cole (d. 1757), merchant and president of the Tuesday Club, was also an enthusiastic singer. Like Thornton, he knew a large repertoire of British songs and was adept at fitting existing melodies to new words.[91] He must have been a tenor, and a nasal one at that. Hamilton's humorous account of Cole's musicianship and description of his voice reads as follows:

> His knowledge in music, he has merely by force of genius, having never been taught, and his talent this way lies in vocal execution, he having a number of old songs by him, the words of which, he affirms, he never is at a loss to find a tune, and indeed, give him words at any time, and he'll immediately clap a tune to them, with so sweet and small a voice, and so delicate a trill, that some people have doubted whether or not he has in his youth been Italianized, but be that as it will . . . he has a most exquisite pipe, and, were he not obliged sometimes to wear his spectacles, to read the words of the song, when he sings by book, his voice would be quite clear, and without asperity, but this nasal machine, will sometimes in the high notes, occasion a snuffling, which a nice ear will easily excuse, seeing the cause is known to proceed from no natural defect.[92]

This attribution of Cole's nasal timbre to the spectacles that pinched his nose must be one of history's most diplomatic musical criticisms.

Cole also composed verses and tunes. Hamilton, writing of the president's singing of "Whilst I Gaze on Chloe, Trembling," continued, "He had a poetical genius, and had added several verses to that ancient song with his own accurate hand." Hamilton noted that Cole sang his sad verses with such emotion that the members wept; it was, however, impossible to determine if the tears were from grief or laughter.[93] The president sang often from an unidentified book of songs that he carried in his pocket.[94] He composed at least one melody, described as "an excellent new tune of his own setting with a proper Chorus."[95] This song was a setting of Jonas Green's poetical mock trial of a seller of ill-fitting shoes (see chap. 5, song 27).

William Lux (d. 1778) was a native of Anne Arundel County, Maryland. In September 1751 he advertised "European Goods" for sale in the *Maryland Gazette*,[96] and on November 26 of that year, he was a guest in the Tuesday Club: "Mr. Wm. Lux, a gentleman Invited to the Club, by permission of his Lordship and the members, Sung the following Song Composed in honor of his Lordship and the Club, while the Secretary play'd the Symphony *Con violoncello Solo*."[97] This passage illustrates an important point concerning the use of the term *composed*, which, in this context, actually means "adapted" (a practice already noted in this book). The club's history, describing the same sederunt, states that Lux sang this song to the tune of "Come Jolly Bacchus" (see chap. 5, song 21).[98]

Lux was also the club's only keyboard instrumentalist; club documents show that he played both harpsichord and organ.[99] He was a frequent guest, playing or singing at sederunts 168, 169, 172, 173, 175, 177, the club's seventh anniversary on May 12, 1752, and at sederunt 195, when he accompanied Hamilton and Malcolm on the organ. Lux entered the club as a regular member on April 3, 1753.[100] The instruments on which he performed were probably his own; in addition to his being the only keyboard performer noted in club documents, he was the only club member to advertise such instruments in the *Maryland Gazette*.[101] After the demise of the Tuesday Club, Lux's continued support of the arts is evident in a petition that he signed requesting Governor Horatio Sharpe to institute a levy to provide for an organist at St. Paul's Parish, Baltimore.[102]

Following his years of activity in the Tuesday Club, Lux emerged as one of Maryland's most prosperous citizens. He had begun to build his fortune while serving the colonial government as deputy to the Collector of His Majesty's Duties at Patapsco in 1751,[103] thereby assisting James Sterling, a figure whose Tuesday Club connections have already been noted (see p. 10). His later activities centered in Baltimore County, where he was married in 1752.[104] At the time of his death, his estate included forty-one slaves and was valued at 43,561 pounds sterling, an enormous sum.[105]

Many other members and guests, such as Green, Lomas, Hart, Wollaston, Daniel Dulany, Jr., and Bullen, were musically active in the club, but their music making was more occasional than that of the musicians discussed in this chapter. The contribution of these "occasional" musicians will be noted in the following chapter.

NOTES

1. Elaine G. Breslaw, ed., *Records of the Tuesday Club of Annapolis, 1745–56* (Urbana: University of Illinois Press, 1988), sederunt 1, May 14, 1745.

2. Ibid., sederunt 12, July 30, 1745; sederunt 252, Feb. 10, 1756.

3. Upton Scott, letter to Library Company of Baltimore, 1809, transcribed in Breslaw, ed., *Records*.

4. Alexander Hamilton, "The History of the Ancient and Honorable Tuesday Club," 3 vols., The Johns Hopkins University Library and Maryland Historical Society, Baltimore, 2:505; Breslaw, ed., *Records*, sederunt 171, Jan. 7, 1752.

5. Hamilton, "History" 3:120–38; Breslaw, ed., *Records*, sederunt 188, Oct. 26, 1752.

6. Hamilton, "History" 2:510; Breslaw, ed., *Records*, sederunt 173, Feb. 4, 1752.

7. Hamilton, "History" 2:71; Breslaw, ed., *Records*, sederunt 122, Jan. 16, 1750.

8. Breslaw, ed., *Records*, sederunt 135, July 31, 1750.

9. Ibid., sederunt 124, Feb. 13, 1750.

10. Ibid., sederunt 139, Sept. 18, 1750. Despite the ban the conundrums were occasionally revived, according to Hamilton, "History" 3:189.

11. Breslaw, ed., *Records*, sederunt 105, May 16, 1749.

12. For a detailed discussion of this particular aspect of Tuesday Club humor, see Elaine G. Breslaw, "Wit, Whimsy, and Politics: The Uses of Satire by the Tuesday Club of Annapolis, 1744[5] to 1756," *William and Mary Quarterly*, 3d ser., 32 (1975): 295–306.

13. Hamilton, "History" 3:48; Breslaw, ed., *Records*, sederunt 181, June 16, 1752.

14. Hamilton, "History" 2:147, 371.

15. Ibid. 3:217–18; Breslaw, ed., *Records*, sederunt 202, May 15, 1753.

16. Hamilton, "History" 3:218 (18–19).

17. Ibid. 3:549. Cole's song "The Jurors of the City Bring" appears in the fragment of the history held by the Maryland Historical Society, Dulany Papers, MS. 1265; and in Breslaw, ed., *Records*, sederunt 237, Feb. 25, 1755.

18. James R. Heintze, "Malcolm Alexander," *The New Grove Dictionary of Music and Musicians*, ed. Stanley Sadie (London: Macmillan, 1980), 11:568.

19. J. A. Leo Lemay, *Men of Letters in Colonial Maryland* (Knoxville: University of Tennessee Press, 1972), p. 213.

20. Ibid., p. 214; and Alexander Hamilton, letter to Gavin Hamilton, June 13, 1739, Dulany Papers, Maryland Historical Society.

21. Lemay, *Men of Letters*, p. 214.

22. Walter Dulany and Dennis Dulany were members; Daniel Dulany, Jr., was often a guest in the club.

23. "Vestry Proceedings, St. Ann's Parish, Annapolis, Md.," *Maryland Historical Magazine* 9 (1914): 166–69; *Maryland Gazette*, Mar. 1, and Apr. 12, 1753; "Hamilton, Alexander," in Edward Papenfuse et al., *A Biographical Dictionary of the Maryland Legislature* (Baltimore: The Johns Hopkins University Press, 1979), 1:309–10.

24. Alexander Hamilton, *Itinerarium, Being a Narrative of a Journey from Annapolis, Maryland through Delaware, Pennsylvania, New York, New Jersey, Connecticut, Rhode Island, Massachusetts and New Hampshire from May to September, 1744*, ed. Albert Bushnell Hart (St. Louis: Bixby, 1907); also published as *Gentleman's Progress: The Itinerarium of Dr. Alexander Hamilton, 1744*, ed. Carl Bridenbaugh (Chapel Hill: University of North Carolina Press, 1948).

25. Hamilton, *Itinerarium*, p. 25.

26. Ibid., p. 236. "Quin" was a prominent colonial performer; Oscar G. T. Sonneck, *Early Concert-Life in America (1737–1800)* (1907; rpt., New York: Da Capo Press, 1978), p. 159, documents a performance by "Mr. Quin" in the Court Room of City Hall, New York City, Oct. 19, 1749.

27. Hamilton, *Itinerarium*, p. 178.

28. Ibid., pp. 102–3.

29. Ibid., p. 57.

30. Ibid., p. 169.

31. Ibid., pp. 144–45. Alexander Malcolm, *A Treatise of Musick, Speculative, Practical, and Historical* (Edinburgh: n.p., 1721).

32. Hamilton, *Itinerarium*, p. 234.

33. Ibid., p. 218.

34. Ibid., p. 134.

35. Ibid., pp. 28–29.

36. Ibid., p. 85. See also Dena J. Epstein, *Sinful Tunes and Spirituals: Black Folk Music to the Civil War* (Urbana: University of Illinois Press, 1977), pp. 147–48; and Charles Hamm, *Music in the New World* (New York: W. W. Norton, 1983), pp. 123–25.

37. *Maryland Gazette*, Feb. 4, 1746. The satire includes a prescription for the cure of "Furor Poeticus" and "Febris Amatoria" by "Polypharmacus, M.D."

38. Attributed to Hamilton by Lemay, *Men of Letters*, p. 230.

39. Hamilton, "History" 1 : 1.

40. Ibid., pp. 7, 25, and 31, respectively.

41. Ibid., pp. 37–38.

42. Ibid., pp. x–xi.

43. A transcription of the history, edited by Robert A. Micklus, will soon be published by the Institute for Early American History and Culture.

44. Breslaw, ed., *Records*, sederunt 252, Feb. 10, 1756.

45. *Maryland Gazette*, May 13, 1756.

46. The entire letter appears in Hamilton, *Itinerarium*, pp. xv–xvi.

47. Lemay, *Men of Letters*, p. 314. For an account of Bacon written by a contemporary biographer, see Jonathan Boucher's footnote in William Hutchinson, *History of the County of Cumberland* (Carlisle, England: n.p., 1794), 2 : 41n. Other valuable references are Ethan Allen, "Rev. Thomas Bacon," *American Quarterly Church Review* 17 (Oct. 1865): 470; Samuel A. Harrison and Oswald Tilghman, *History of Talbot County, Maryland* (Baltimore: William and Wilkins, 1915), 1 : 278–79; Lawrence C. Wroth, *A History of Printing in Colonial Maryland* (Baltimore: Typothetae, 1922), pp. 95–110; and William E. Deibert, "Thomas Bacon, Colonial Clergyman," *Maryland Historical Magazine* 73 (1978): 79–86.

48. Thomas Bacon, *A Compleat System of the Revenue of Ireland, in Its Several Branches of Import, Export, and Inland Duties* (Dublin: Reilly, 1737); Lemay, *Men of Letters*, p. 314.

49. Lemay, *Men of Letters*, pp. 315–16.

50. Samuel Richardson, *The History of Sir Charles Grandison* (London: author, 1754), 7 : 441.

51. Announcing the first public performance of *Messiah*.

52. Lemay, *Men of Letters*, p. 316, observed that, since the same notice appeared in the *Dublin Gazette*, Bacon may not have written it.

53. Ibid., pp. 317–18.

54. Harrison and Tilghman, *Talbot County* 1 : 79.

55. Deibert, "Thomas Bacon," p. 79.

56. Thomas Bacon, *Laws of Maryland at Large* (Annapolis: Green, 1765); Lemay, *Men of Letters*, pp. 313–18. A checklist of Bacon's publications appears in Lemay, *Men of Letters*, pp. 382–87.

57. Thomas Bacon, *Four Sermons, Preached at the Parish Church of St. Peter, in Talbot County, in the Province of Maryland . . . Viz. Two Sermons to Black Slaves, and Two Sermons for the Benefit of a Charity Working-School, in the Above Parish, for the Maintenance and Education of Orphans and Poor Children and Negroes* (London: Oliver, 1753). The *Maryland Gazette*, on Sept. 19, 1750, advertised a proposal for Bacon's school, to be established for the educa-

tion of poor children and Negroes. The titles of several of Bacon's sermons concerning education for slaves and for the poor are included in Lemay's checklist of publications (*Men of Letters*, pp. 382–85).

58. Thomas Bacon, "An Account of What Passed at a Meeting of the Clergy at Annapolis in October 1753, with Other Matters Relating Thereto," *Maryland Historical Magazine* 2 (1908): 364–84.

59. *Maryland Gazette*, June 12, 1751, gives a progress report on the school, listing some of the supporters; and ibid., Apr. 19, 1752, announced that plans for the school could be seen at Dr. Alexander Hamilton's pharmacy.

60. Ibid., Oct. 2, 1751 (Annapolis concert); Oct. 12, 1752 (Upper Marlborough concert); Dec. 14, 1752 (Annapolis theater benefit); and Dec. 19, 1754 (Williamsburg concert). Also see Lemay, *Men of Letters*, p. 322.

61. Harrison and Tilghman, *History of Talbot County* 2:488; Governor Horatio Sharpe, letter to Frederick Calvert, Lord Baltimore, May 23, 1760, *Archives of Maryland*, vol. 9 (Baltimore: Maryland Historical Society, 1890), p. 445.

62. *Maryland Gazette*, Apr. 8, 1756. Bacon's son has been erroneously reported as drowned at sea in Wroth, *History of Printing in Colonial Maryland*, p. 97; and Deibert, "Thomas Bacon," p. 81. Even Lemay, *Men of Letters*, pp. 333–34, is confusing on the date of Jacky's death, giving it as 1756.

63. Wroth, *History of Printing in Colonial Maryland*, pp. 96–97.

64. Lemay, *Men of Letters*, p. 335.

65. Thomas Bacon, letter to Henry Callister, Mar. 1757, Callister Papers, Maryland Diocesan Archives, Baltimore.

66. Lemay, *Men of Letters*, p. 337.

67. Bacon owned a harpsichord at the time of his death. Frederick County Inventories, 1769, box 6, folder 38.

68. W. H. Grattan Flood, "Eighteenth Century Italians in Dublin," *Music & Letters* 3 (1922): 274–78.

69. Thomas Bacon, "See, See, My Boys," *The Gentleman's Catch Book* ([Dublin:] Mountain, [1786]), p. 25

70. Hutchinson, *History of the County of Cumberland* 2:41n.

71. Hamilton, "History" 3:241.

72. Lemay, *Men of Letters*, p. 342; Walter Muir Whitehill, *Independent Historical Societies* (Boston: Boston Athenaeum, 1962), pp. 113–14.

73. *Maryland Gazette*, June 9, 1768; *Virginia Gazette*, June 23, 1768; *Pennsylvania Chronicle*, June 13, 1768.

74. James R. Heintze, "Alexander Malcolm: Musician, Clergyman, and Schoolmaster," *Maryland Historical Magazine* 73 (1978): 226–29. Other valuable references for Malcolm are Maurer Maurer, "Alexander Malcolm in America," *Music & Letters* 33 (1952): 226; and Reppard Stone, "An Evaluative Study of Alexander Malcolm's 'Treatise of Music: Speculative, Practical and Historical'" (Ph.D. diss., Catholic University, 1974), pp. 1–23.

75. Hamilton, *Itinerarium*, p. 145.

76. Ibid., pp. 146–49.

77. *Vital Records of Marblehead, Massachusetts to the End of the Year 1849* (Salem, Mass.: Essex Institute, 1904), 2:276.

78. For a historical and theoretical analysis of Malcolm's *Treatise*, see Stone, "An Evaluative Study," pp. 25–90.

79. *Archives of Maryland*, vol. 6 (Baltimore: Maryland Historical Society, 1888), pp. 9, 54.

80. Breslaw, ed., *Records*, sederunt 222, June 11, 1754; Hamilton, "History" 3: 371–77. Both documents include Malcolm's farewell speech to the club.

81. "Queen Anne's County Free School Minute Book," MS. 683, pp. 90, 93, 95–98, Manuscripts Division, Maryland Historical Society.

82. "St. Paul's Parish Register," vol. 2, p. 13, Maryland Hall of Records, Annapolis, Md.

83. *Maryland Gazette*, June 30, 1763.

84. Ibid., Apr. 8, 1746, "Sheriff"; mercantile activities in ibid., Nov. 11, 1746, and Jan. 16, 1751; obituary, Feb. 3, 1769. Thornton's birthdate remains unknown.

85. Hamilton, "History" 1:281.

86. Breslaw, ed., *Records*, sederunt 49, Nov. 25, 1746; Hamilton, "History" 1:283, describes the requirement that Thornton sing his votes.

87. Breslaw, ed., *Records*, sederunt 124, Feb. 13, 1750; and Hamilton, "History" 2:97, show that Thornton was censured for attempting to play the fiddle.

88. Hamilton, "History" 3:218 (18–19).

89. Breslaw, ed., *Records*, sederunt 105, May 16, 1749. The claim of several historians that Samuel Hart played the flute is probably based on this passage. Hamilton's term "delicate pipe," however, was invariably used to compliment a voice rather than a musical instrument (see pp. 49 and 59).

90. Ibid., sederunt 163, Sept. 3, 1751.

91. *Maryland Gazette*, July 7, 1757. Cole's obituary states that he had resided in Annapolis for over forty years. His familiarity with English songs suggests that he was English, and, as president of the club, he was probably among its older members. If he arrived in Annapolis in his twenties, he would have been in his fifties when he entered the club and in his sixties at the time of his death, which places his birth in the last decade of the seventeenth century.

92. Hamilton, "History" 1:162.

93. Ibid., p. 163.

94. Ibid., p. 339.

95. Ibid. 3:549; Breslaw, ed., *Records*, sederunt 237, Feb. 25, 1755.

96. *Maryland Gazette*, Sept. 4, 1751.

97. Breslaw, ed., *Records*, sederunt 168, Nov. 26, 1751.

98. Hamilton, "History" 2:452; Breslaw, ed., *Records*, sederunt 169, Dec. 10, 1751.

99. Breslaw, ed., *Records*, sederunt 169, Dec. 10, 1751.

100. Ibid., sederunt 199, Apr. 3, 1753.

101. *Maryland Gazette*, July 28, 1763; June 14, 1764; Aug. 8, 1765.

102. An abstract of the petition with the names of the signers is in *Calendar of Maryland State Papers, No. 1, The Black Books* (Annapolis: State of Maryland Publications of the Hall of Records Commission, 1943), p. 189. The date is listed as "after 1763."

103. *Maryland Gazette*, Sept. 4, 1751; and Donnell M. Owings, *His Lordship's Patronage* (Baltimore: Maryland Historical Society, 1953), p. 182, an excellent source, explaining exactly how various colonial offices functioned.

104. "Lux, William," in Papenfuse et al., *A Biographical Dictionary of the Maryland Legislature* 2:556–57; "St. Paul's Parish Records," vol. 1, p. 109, microfilm 994, Maryland Hall of Records, Annapolis, Md.

105. "Baltimore County Inventories," vol. 12 (1781), p. 239, Maryland Hall of Records, Annapolis, Md.

5

SONGS, ODES, AND INCIDENTAL MUSIC OF THE TUESDAY CLUB

Hamilton's Essay on Music

Alexander Hamilton's views on music and its role in the Tuesday Club are set forth in his "History of the Ancient and Honorable Tuesday Club," volume 3, chapter 8:

> Music is an art, or (as some have been pleased to call it,) a science, which has been condemn'd or applauded, according to men's different fancies; for my part I believe it is neither good nor bad, considered in itself simply, but Diogenes and Plato among the ancients seem to be of contrary opinions concerning it. The first, as a cynic, told a certain person, who bragged of his skill in music, that cities and states were governed by wisdom, but that a small family could not be kept in order by fiddling and a song; the latter, as an academic, the principles of whose philosophy were more generous and enlarged, compares the symmetry and order of the heavenly bodies to a chorus and audience, and to music & harmony and the comparison in the opinion of many is Just and Elegant, and the same divine philosopher says somewhere in his writings ["For harmony and concord and number naturally come to be in many things"].[1]
>
> Our modern Italians are so biggotted to the excellency of this art, that they have a maxim, whoever Loves not Music, is not beloved of God, the ancient Hebrews used music in their devotion, as we may see by the stories transmitted to us of king David and his harp, which had the power of charming the evil spirit from Saul; the Greeks used it in war, and we find an instance of the Spartans being fond of it for that purpose, but then, they were for confining it to a certain compass, and therefore imposed a fine on Terpander and nailed his harp to a post, for adding one

string to the number before used; by Orpheus's music is understood the establishment of politeness, peace and morality among
men, for, by the power of his modulations he civilized the Satyrs,
who were properly the unpolished part of the human species
which ranged the woods with their kindred brutes, and, it is certain we are told in the sacred Archives that Alleluias, and Celes-
tial hymns are sung in heaven;—yet, notwithstanding all these
great authorities in favor of music, many Heroes and Sages have
esteemed it a triffling, unmanly and scandalous science. Philip of
Macedon, asked his son Alexander, if he was not ashamed of his
singing so well. Themistocles being asked, if he could play on the
harp, said, he did not know, he never had tried, but, that he
knew very well how to plan a battle or storm a town, these being
arts he was practised in. Salust the Roman Historian speaking of
the qualifications of a courtesan, says that she did, *Psaltere et Sal-
tare elegantius quam necesse est proba* [to sing and to dance more
elegantly than necessary is a good thing], yet certain it is, notwithstanding the contempt with which many have treated this
elegant art, and its professors (a good fidler being now a days
looked upon with scorn, as having spent much time in acquiring
a triffling accomplishment, if any accomplishment be called triffling), that some of the wisest and greatest men have been captivated
with it. Stratonice with a song entraped Mithridates to her hive,
and held him as fast as a bird in a cage, and tho' the honorable
Mr. President Jole, and his Longstanding members, had the
character of wise, judicious, grave and great men, yet were they
captivated to a great degree with the musical performances of
Signr. Lardini Musician Con Stromenti to the Club, so as to
show the greatest signs of rapture and extacy, when that artist
performed on his fiddle, the music of the Anniversary Odes,
and Songs of the Club, but, from this, I will not presume to con-
clude, that the members of this Club were Platonists, or of the
academic sect, for had it been so, they would, like Plato have
banished music from their common wealth, neither did they use
music on the account of religion or war, but perhaps might intend to polish, soften, and humanize their rough and savage
LgStand. members [longstanding = regular members] if any
such might possibly be, or come among them.[2]

Hamilton acknowledged music's detractors but defended the art as a
civilizing force. Although his style is typically satirical, the essay is probably a true statement of the author's philosophy, which did not take music
too seriously. Hamilton and his friends were dilettantes, not artists; al-

though their music, especially Bacon's, displays skill and sophistication, they were more concerned with style than with substance. Music for them was a pleasant diversion and a happy reminder of the social and cultural activities they had enjoyed in the British Isles.

Songs

Twenty-eight songs and catches appear in the extant Tuesday Club documents; most were popular music of the period. Some were well-known tunes for which the club members wrote new lyrics, and at least one was composed by a club member. The songs are presented here in order of their appearance in Hamilton's history of the Tuesday Club.

Robert Gordon, one of the founders of the club, sang the catch "Merry Meet, and Merry Part" at the club's inaugural meeting on May 14, 1745. Hamilton's description of the music performed on this occasion follows: "This first sederunt was finished in a gay and jovial manner, by the singing of several ancient catches, at which Capt. Serious Social [Robert Gordon] was a good hand, and sung the following, holding up a large punch bowl well replenished, which I think worthy of a place in this history, because it became afterwards a Constant Club Catch."[3]

1. "Merry Meet, and Merry Part"

Merry meet and merry part,
Here's to thee with all my heart.
One bowl in hand, and another in store,
Enough's enough, and we'll have one more.

Source: Hamilton, "History" 1:143–44. No other sources are known to exist. All major published eighteenth-century catch collections have been searched as well as the extensive published and manuscript song and catch collections of the Library of Congress and the British Library.

The singing of catches, particularly those pertaining to drinking, was a popular pastime. Robert Gordon also hosted the club's third meeting on May 28, 1745, and introduced a similar catch, "Signior Domingo." Everyone apparently sang, since the catch "went round the members."[4]

2. "Signior Domingo; or,
There Was a Man of Very Great Fame"

There was a man of very great fame
Signior Domingo was his name.
He was a man not given to quarrel,
But now and then, with a sma'beer barrel
And, when he died, he was so kind,
As to leave this very bowl for us behind.

Source: Hamilton, "History" 1 : 144–45. No other source is known.

Two lines from the song "Auld Rob Morris" were used in a disparaging description of Charles Cole:

Auld Rob Morris, I ken him fou well,
His arse it sticks out like ony peet creel.[5]

Hamilton merely quoted this excerpt in his history; there is no evidence that the song was actually sung in the club. I include it here because "Auld Rob Morris" was undoubtedly well known to Hamilton and his friends. It appeared in *Musick for Allan Ramsay's Collection of Scots Songs* (the book of songs probably ordered by Henry Callister in 1744) and in Henry Roberts's *Calliope*, a collection that included no less than six of the Tuesday Club songs.[6]

3. "Auld Rob Morris"

There's old Rob Mor-ris, that wons in—yon glen, He's the
King o'— guid fal - lows, and wale o'— auld men; He has

four-score o'— black sheep, and four-score ___ too; And ___

auld ___ Rob Mor-ris is the man ye— maun lo'e.

Source: The music was copied from *Musick for Allan Ramsay's Collection of Scots Songs* (Edinburgh: Ramsay, ca. 1726), pp. 116–17; the complete text appears in Robert Chambers, ed., *The Songs of Scotland prior to Burns* (Edinburgh: Chambers, 1862), pp. 210–12.

"Whilst I Gaze on Chloe, Trembling" existed in two versions during the Tuesday Club era. The form given below, set by Lewis Ramondon, is the earlier, appearing in Watts's *Musical Miscellany* of 1729 as "The Lukewarm Lover."[7] The tune was also heard in several ballad operas, notably *The Devil to Pay* (1731), which was performed in Annapolis in 1752.[8] The original text was set to a new tune by Digard, published in Bickham's *Musical Entertainer* of ca. 1737.[9] Although Digard's setting cannot be ruled out, Ramondon's version is more commonly encountered in the major eighteenth-century sources and is probably the melody that was familiar to the Tuesday Club. Charles Cole added some original verses enjoyed by club members:

> Whilst I gaze on Cloe trembling

which song in the printed editions wants about twelve or 15 stanzas, which Mr. Jole used to sing to the tune. This induced some to believe, tho' Mr. Jole never showed it, or seemed to be vain of it, that he had a poetical genius, and had added several verses to that ancient song with his own accurate hand. Some of these verses are in themselves very sublime and poetical, one of which, for its beauty and singularity, I cannot ommit here quoting.

> Here there lies Interr'd a Squire
> Underneath this marble stone.

Who for Loving did expire,
And he never Lov'd but one.

This verse in particular Mr. Jole would sing with so lamentable a voice, as to draw tears from the eyes of the most flinty hearted, tho' many assumed that these tears flowed not from commiseration, but from a certain gelastic conquassation [laughter].[10]

4. "Whilst I Gaze on Chloe, Trembling"

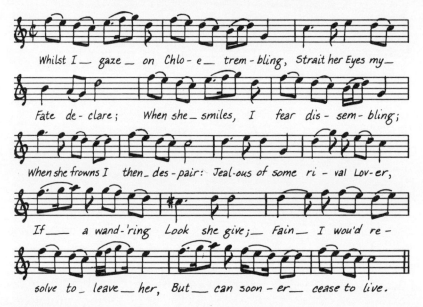

Source: Both the music and text were copied from *The Musical Miscellany*, vol. 2 (London: Watts, 1729), p. 76.

———

Yet another drinking catch, "The Great Bell of Lincoln," was a ceremonial piece, ordered by club law 15 to be sung at the admission of each new member. It was first performed on July 23, 1745, in the following manner: "The great bell of Lincoln was sung for the first time by Nasifer Jole Esqr. [Charles Cole] a large bowl of Rack punch being carried in procession Round the Great table, typically representing the great bell, while the members followed in Regular order, shouldering tobacco pipes. This was the first appearance of pomp and pageantry, in this ancient and honorable club."[11] Hamilton's performance directions for this catch are given below exactly as they were recorded with the text of "The Great Bell":

The great Bell of Lincoln
It rings once a year,
But we're not for Lincoln
While this Bell rings here[a]

Chorus:
There are five men to raise her[b]
and at whitsontide rings
Then turn the bell over
and see how she rings[c]

Now the bell is turn'd over
and has lost her old strings
and she must be mended
before she will ring

New frame, new wheel,
new clapper, new strings
Then turn the bell over
and see how she rings.

Chorus:
Drink right, or else your wrong
Poor Tom is dead and gone
To——m, T——m

[a]here they sound upon the bowl with a tobacco pipe
[b]here 5 take hold of the bowl, and raise it up high in the air
[c]here they drink.

5. "The Great Bell of Lincoln"

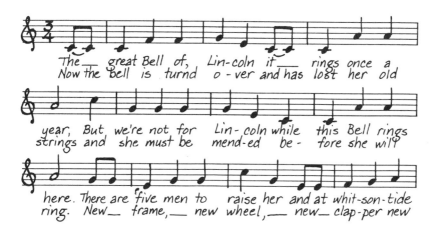

The— great Bell of, Lin-coln it— rings once a
Now the bell is turnd o-ver and has lost her old

year, But we're not for Lin-coln while this Bell rings
strings and she must be mend-ed be-fore she will

here. There are five men to raise her and at whit-son-tide
ring. New— frame,— new wheel,— new— clap-per new

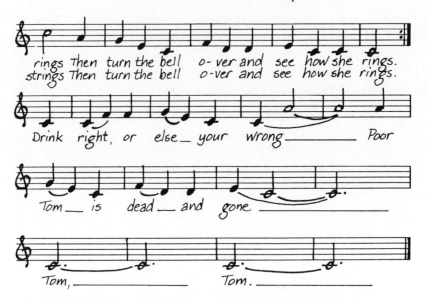

rings Then turn the bell o-ver and see how she rings.
strings Then turn the bell o-ver and see how she rings.

Drink right, or else__ your wrong_____ Poor

Tom__ is dead__ and gone _____

Tom,_____ Tom._____

Source: The words of the song with Hamilton's annotations appear in Hamilton, "History" 1:169. No contemporaneous tune source has come to light. The tune given here is from the "George Butterworth MS," vol. 6(b), p. 8, text only in vol. 4, p. 223, in the Library of the English Folk Dance and Song Society, London. This tune was recorded in 1907 by Butterworth, as sung by a Mr. George Knight of Horsham. The complete text given by Butterworth is an almost exact version of lines 9–16 of Hamilton's "Bell." Fitting Hamilton's text to the Butterworth tune is made difficult by the closing three lines, designated in the history as "Chorus." I have arbitrarily set them to the first two musical phrases and suggest that the piece end with a repeated bell tone, typical of other "bell" catches. The piece, as it appears here, is not a catch at all but a simple toast; however, with a few alterations in measures 1, 14, and 15, the song could be performed as a two-, three-, or four-part round, and that may well be the original form of the piece. Additionally, a bell tone on C (To——m, T——m) could sound through the entire catch as a drone. Hamilton probably did not use the term *chorus* in a structural sense, but simply to indicate passages to be sung by more than one singer.

———

During the winter of 1745–46, several Tuesday Club members engaged in a curious poetry contest with two "Baltimore Bards," who had composed a poem that compared the influence of the famous Reverend George Whitefield's sermon to the emotions stirred by the beauty of the young ladies seated just in front of the poets.[12] A manuscript copy of the poem reached the Tuesday Club; Hamilton and his friends responded with a formal critique, thus beginning a literary battle that included exchanges of poetry, insults, and suggested remedies for the cure of bad poetry. Several of these items actually appeared in the *Maryland Gazette*,[13] and the complete story is preserved in Hamilton's history.[14] One of the products of this battle of wits was the following song, which was probably written by Hamilton, Edward Dorsey, the Reverend John Gordon, Witham Marshe, and John Bullen.[15] Although no tune is specified, the song can be set to numerous melodies, including "Orpheus and Euridice," which was familiar to the Tuesday Club (see song 10). The song's suggestion that these Baltimore clergymen were much attracted to worldly pleasures is typical of the period.

6. "Song on the Baltimore Bards"

Ye Baltimore Bards, while your fame we rehearse,
   The muses we cannot invoke.
Since we ne'er should expect they would dictate our verse
   While singing so errant a joke.

This too would resemble some clerks of our day,
   Who act as absurdly as think,
In the morning on Sundays they preach & they pray,
   In the evening they sing and they drink.

Say, wonderful bards, how your muse is inspir'd?
   By what magic power does she sing.
By the Demon or Moorfields, or punch is she fir'd
   For she drinks not the Helicon Spring.

Say, does she not soar to a wonderful height
   In clubs of our raking gallants,
When o'er punch and Tobacco on Sundays at night
   The cuckold and Cuckoo she chants.

To the Tune of the Cuckold, pray chant it no more
   for on this I will venture my oath
Your slut of a muse will turn out common whore
   and shortly will Cuckold you both.

As Cuckolds are hooted and scoff'd in the streets
   for their horns, so may you for your wit.
Rank fools you appear by your billingsgate Sheets
   and your Poems shall soon be b——s——t.

Source: Hamilton, "History" 1 : 190. No tune is specified.

———————

"Rev. Smoothum Sly" (Reverend John Gordon) sang a Scots song, "Hooly and Fairly," at the twelfth meeting on July 30, 1745. The text is given as it appears in Hamilton's history of the Tuesday Club; the tune is from

Robert Bremner's *Thirty Scots Songs*, printed in 1757.[16] *The National Tune Index* cites *The Philosopher's Opera* (1757) as an early source, and Chambers's *Songs of Scotland* traces it as far back as "Yair's Charmer" (1751).[17] Hamilton's account of its performance in 1745, written in 1754 or 1755, provides one of the earliest recorded versions of the text.

7. "Hooly and Fairly"

Source: The tune was copied from *Thirty Scots Songs* (Edinburgh: Robert Bremner, [1757]), p. 41; the words are recorded as they appear in Hamilton, "History" 1 : 192–93. "Hooly and Fairly" means "in moderation."

Another Scots song, "Jog Hooly Good Man," was contributed by "Capt. Serious Social" (Robert Gordon) on August 20, 1745.[18] The precise meaning of the term *jog* in this context is unclear; *hooly* means "softly, graciously, or courteously."

8. "Jog Hooly Good Man"

Jog hooly good man, or the bed'il fa,
Jog hooly good man, or the bed'il fa,
The bed is made of rotten timmer
And if it fa's it'l smoor our good mither
And she'll cry out and shame us a'
Jog hooly good man or the bed'il fa,
The bed, its tied at head and feet,
With simmer won hay and that's right sweet,
And in comes the crummie cow she eats it a,
Jog hooly good man or the bed'il fa.

Source: Hamilton, "History" 1 : 196. No other source is known.

———————

In describing William Thornton's singing of "When Cloe We Ply," Hamilton suggests that a variety of tunes were utilized for a given song: "At the same Sederunt, Solo Neverout Esqr. [Thornton], being gifted with an excellent voice, entertained the club with a song, which, as it became the subject of frequent trials of skill, between his honor the president and him, which should sing it most musically, *and apply the best air to the words,* we shall here give a transcript of it" (emphasis added).[19] This practice of "applying the best air" to a given text was evidently common in the Tuesday Club and was typical of the era, providing, as it were, the musical basis of the ballad opera. The song is reproduced here using the text from the history, with the melody that accompanies the same words in Watts's *Musical Miscellany.*

9. "When Cloe We Ply; or, 'Tis Artifice All"

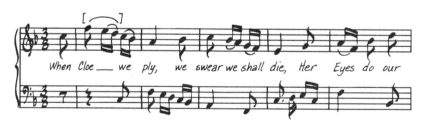

When Cloe ___ we ply, we swear we shall die, Her Eyes do our

Note: Brackets indicate suggested modifications needed to accommodate the Tuesday Club version of text.

The maidens are coy
They'll pish, and they'll fie
and swear if you're rude they will bawl,
But they whisper so low
by which you may know

'Tis artifice, artifice all, all, all
'Tis artifice, artifice all.

The wives they will cry
My dear, if you die,
To marry again I ne'er shall
But less than a year
Will make it appear

'Tis artifice, etc.

In matters of State
and party debate
For Church and for Justice they'll bawl,
But if you'll attend
You'll find in the end

'Tis artifice, artifice all, all, all
'Tis artifice, artifice all.

Source: The tune was copied from *The Musical Miscellany*, vol. 3 (London: Watts, 1730), p. 81; the words are cited as they appear in Hamilton, "History" 1 : 281–82.

Thornton, the Anne Arundel County sheriff and musician "con Voce" of the Tuesday Club, was a favorite target for club humor and was often accused of breaking various club laws. On June 23, 1747, he was charged with "negligence in his office," and he responded by introducing two new songs, "Orpheus and Euridice" and "The Pleasures of Life." The club enjoyed these contributions so much that they voted Thornton the right to require any member to sing, including the president, after Thornton himself had first performed. Predictably, this act occasioned another constitutional debate concerning the propriety of enacting legislation governing the conduct of the president, who was thought to be above the law.[20]

10. "Orpheus and Euridice"

When Orph-eus went down to the re-gions be-low,___ Which men are for-bid-den to___ see,___ He tuned up his lyre, as old his-to-ries show, to set his Eu-rid-i-ce free ___ To

set his Eu-rid-i-ce free.___ All hell was sur-priz'd that a

per-son so___ wise, should rash-ly en-dan-ger his life;___ But,

o, ye good gods, how vast their sur-prise when they knew that he came for___ his___

wife,___ how___ vast their sur-prise, when they knew that he___ came for his wife.___

Source: The song is by William Boyce and was copied from *Universal Harmony* (London: Newberry, 1745), p. 34; the words are reproduced as they appear in Hamilton, "History" 1:314–15.

Thornton's second tune of the evening combined the club's favorite song subjects—women and wine.

11. "The Pleasures of Life; or, Save Women and Wine"

Save wom-en & wine there is noth-ing in life ___ can ___ bribe hon-est souls to en-

dure it, save wom-en & wine, there's noth-ing in life __ can bribe hon-est souls to en-

dure it. When the heart is tor-ment – ed with care & with strife, __ Dear

wom-en & wine on-ly cure __ it. When it heart is tor-ment-ed with care & with strife, dear

wom-en & wine, sweet wom-en & wine, Dear wom-en & wine on-ly cure it.

Note: Brackets in the following stanzas indicate text repetitions that have been restored to facilitate reading with the music.

Come on my brave boys, we'll have women and wine,
  and wisely to purpose employ them
[Come on my brave boys, we'll have women and wine,
  and wisely to purpose employ them]
He's a fool that refuses such blessings divine,
  [Who has vigor and health to enjoy them.
He's a fool that refuses such blessings divine
  as women and wine, sweet women and wine,]
Who has vigor and health to enjoy them.

Our wine shall be old, and so my dear Jack,
  To heighten our amorous fire
[Our wine shall be old, and so my dear Jack,
  To heighten our amorous fire]

Our girls plump and sound, they will kiss
with a smack, [And gratify every desire.
Our girls plump and sound, they will kiss
with a smack, our bottles will crack, our
lasses will smack,] And gratify every desire.

Source: The tune was copied from *Calliope; or, English Harmony*, vol. 1 (London: Roberts, 1739), p. 147; the text is from Hamilton, "History" 1:315–16.

———————

Charles Cole sang the song "Where Are You Going" at the final meeting of 1747, after first becoming intoxicated and engaging in a singing contest with Thornton. Hamilton wrote: "His honor the president . . . got so bungy, as the phrase is, that after having outsung Mr. Protomusicus, and beat him at his own weapons, in the celebrated club song of *When Cloe we ply*, he sung a favorite song of his own to the club, with great humor and glee, together with many others. . . ."[21] This selection is typical of the club's love of bawdry.

12a. "Where Are You Going My Pritty Maid"

12b. "Dabbling in the Dew"

sir, she said, I'm going a-milk-ing, sir, she said.
sir, she said, You're kind-ly wel-come, sir, she said.

What if I lay you down, my pritty maid?
Why then you must cover me, Sir, she said,
I thank you kindly my pritty maid
You're kindly welcome, Sir, she said.

But should I get you with Child my pritty maid?
Why then you must father it, Sir, she said,
I thank you kindly my pritty maid,
You're kindly welcome, Sir, she said.

But I will not marry you, my pritty maid
I never desir'd you, Sir, she said.
I thank you kindly my pritty maid,
You're kindly welcome, Sir, she said.

Sources: Song 12a, a round, is attributed to Purcell in Mary Catherine Taylor and Carol Dyk, eds., *The Book of Rounds* (New York: Dutton, 1977), p. 6, but utilizes only the first two lines of the text appearing in Hamilton, "History" 1:339. A Henry Purcell attribution is questionable, since the round does not appear in the twenty-second volume of the Purcell Society, *Catches and Rounds,* ed. William Barclay Squire (London: Purcell Society, 1922), and is not to be found in any of the major eighteenth-century sources, including the catch collections of Playford, Walsh, and Warren. Furthermore, Henry Purcell's bawdy catches are far more complex than this very simple round.

Song 12b is one of ten versions of "Dabbling in the Dew" in Maud Karpeles, ed., *Cecil Sharp's Collection of English Folk Songs* (London: Oxford, 1974), 1:442. This particular version was selected because of its similarity to the Tuesday Club text, which is reproduced here in its entirety from Hamilton, "History" 1:339.

Another drinking round was sung by William Thornton on the club's third anniversary, May 17, 1748:

13. "Trumpet Air"

The king's health, the kings health,
let the trumpet sound,
and the glass go round
Huzza! Huzza! Huzza!

To the downfall of usurpation,
and I long to see the day,
confusion to him
who would set it up again,
Huzza! Huzza! Huzza!

Source: The text is from Hamilton, "History" 1:360–61, where it is entitled "Trumpet Air." *The National Tune Index* lists four distinct tunes under the title "Trumpet Air"; they appear in the following collections: *A Selection of Scotch, English, Irish, and Foreign Airs* (Glasgow: Aird, 1782), 1:67; John H. Ives, "Musical Copybook" (New Haven: Connecticut Historical Society, ca. 1800); *Musica Bellicosa* (London: Walsh, 1733), pp. 17–18; and *Pills to Purge Melancholy*, vol. 2 (London: Tonson, 1719–20), pp. 83–85. The "Trumpet Air" found in *Pills* has a different text and a tune that cannot be easily fitted to the words as they appear in Hamilton's history.

John Bullen entertained the club with the song "To the Hundreds of Drury I Write" on November 8, 1748. Neither the words nor the tune appears in Tuesday Club documents, which simply refer to the piece as "the celebrated old song of the hundreds of Drury" and note its "trolloll" refrain.[22] The song printed here, originally entitled "The Bowman Priggs' Farewell," also features a "Tollol-de rol" refrain; the similarities of the refrain and the first line appear to provide positive identification.

14. "To the Hundreds of Drury I Write"

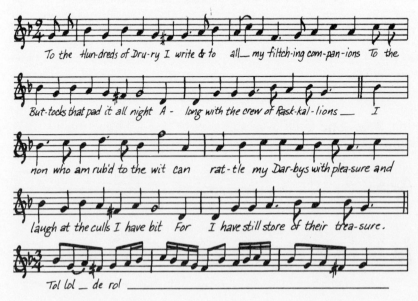

Rat-tle my Dar-by's with plea-sure Tol lol de rol lol de rol.

Source: Harold Gene Moss, "Ballad-Opera Songs: A Record of Ideas Set to Music, 1728–1733" (Ph.D. diss., University of Michigan, 1970), 4:72–73; Moss includes a photographic reproduction of a unique copy dated 1750, now in the British Library.

John Lomas was appointed deputy president for sederunt 102, March 21, 1749, and was required by his commission to sing two specific songs, "Stand Round My Brave Boys" and "Bumpers Squire Jones." Lomas voluntarily added a third song, "She Tells Me, with Claret She Cannot Agree," which Hamilton described as "a favorite of his," and for which he recorded the words in his history. Hamilton suggested that this song represented Lomas's actual views on wine and women:

> The honorable deputy sung this song very pathetically, passion appearing in the twist of his features and glare of his eyes, especially, when he pronounced these words, let her go to the Devil, by which his hearers might easily know, that he was himself a dear lover of his bottle, and this was really the case, for Mr. Comus [Lomas], tho' he would talk but very little upon any subject, yet, when the bowl or bottle came to be the topic of discourse, he held forth very emphatically.[23]

Lomas may have been an alcoholic; he resigned from the club following a meeting in which his mouth was compared to a puppet show—"there is always punch in it."[24] Lomas was truly the club's "Jolly Toper."

15a. "She Tells Me, with Claret She Cannot Agree; or, The Jolly Toper"

she tells me with Clar-et she can-not a-

gree, and she thinks of_ a _ Hogs-head when e're she sees

me, For I smell like a beast and there-fore must

I re - solve to—for- sake her or—Clar-et de-

ny. Must I leave my dear bot-tle that was al-ways my

friend And I hope will con - tin- ue so, to my life's

end, Must I leave it for her, 'tis a ve-ry hard—

task, Let her go to the—Dev- il, [to the

Dev - il] bring— 'toth- er full flask.—

15b. "The Jolly Toper"

She tells me, with Clar- et she can -not a-gree,— and she

thinks of a hogs-head when- e're she sees me,— For I

[a] F-sharp in the original.
[b] The repeat is taken only by the accompaniment.

Must I leave my dear bottle that was always my friend
And I hope will continue so, to my life's end,
Must I leave it for her, 'tis a very hard task,
Let her go to the Devil, bring 'tother full flask.

Had she found out my Chloris, up two pair of stairs,
I had baulk'd her and gone to Saint James's to prayers,
Had she tax'd me with gaming, and bid me forbear,
'Tis a thousand to one, I had lent her an ear.

Had she bid me read homilies, three times a day,
Perhap's she'd been humor'd with little to say,
But at night to deny me, my dear flask of red
Let her go to the Devil, there's no more to be said.

Sources: Thomas Durfey, "The Jolly Toper." There are only two extant copies of single sheet editions, published in London in 1715: Harvard College Library (25242.13, fol. 100) and the British Library (G. 311. 73). Version "a" (song 15a) was copied from the British Library folio. Another tune, also titled "The Jolly Toper," appears in *The Muses Delight* (Liverpool: Sadler, 1754), p. 165, with an entirely different text from that found in Hamilton, "History" 1:422. However, Sadler's tune fits Durfey's words quite effectively. Since the melody published in 1754 was popular during the Tuesday Club years, it may well have been the one heard in the club (song 15b).

———————

The two songs Lomas was required to sing on March 21, 1749, had both appeared in contemporaneous magazines. George Frideric Handel's "Stand Round My Brave Boys" was "made for the Gentlemen Volunteers of the City of London" and was published in the *London Magazine* of November 1745:

16. "Stand Round My Brave Boys"

king, long live the King___ long,___ long live the King, long live the King, &

cho·rus it long live the King.___

Source: London Magazine, Nov. 1745, pp. 560–61. This song is not to be confused with another song of the same title by William Boyce, but subtitled "The Sailor's Return from Cape Breton." Although the battle of Cape Breton was a topic of interest in colonial Annapolis (see the *Maryland Gazette,* Nov. 15, 1745), Boyce's song did not appear until 1758.

The other song Lomas was required to sing was "Bumpers Squire Jones," which had been printed in the *Gentleman's Magazine* for November 1744:

17. "Bumpers Squire Jones; or, Ye Good Fellows All"

Ye good fel·lows all Who love to be told where there's clar-et good store, At-

tend to the call___ of one who's ne'er fright-ed, But great-ly de-light-ed with

Source: Gentleman's Magazine, Nov. 1744, p. 612.

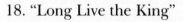

The Tuesday Club records for sederunt 102 add a fourth song, William Boyce's "Long Live the King," to this musical meeting of March 21, 1749. No words or music were recorded, only its title.[25]

18. "Long Live the King"

Long, ___ long, long ___ live ___ the ___ King.

Source: A Collection of Catches, Canons, and Glees, vol. 1 (London: Warren, [1762]), p. 12. Thomas Warren was secretary to the Noblemen and Gentlemen's Catch Club of London. His collection of thirty-two volumes is the most comprehensive eighteenth-century compilation of its kind. This popular round has been published in several collections, with slight variations in its title and first line. It appears in Warren's collection as "Long Live King George," in Rimbault's compilation of 1864 as "Long Live the Queen," and in Taylor and Dyk's modern collection of 1977, bearing the Tuesday Club title. Warren's first line has been altered here to reflect the Tuesday Club title.

On March 26, 1751, Beale Bordley sang the "Boddily Song," which so pleased the members that they gave him exclusive performing rights, ruling that no one, including the president, would be allowed to sing this song. Bordley guarded the words carefully, so as to prevent others from learning the song, and would not give Hamilton a copy; as a result the text has been lost. The song, however, was sung to the "first part" of "Macpherson's Lament," revealing yet another tune familiar to the club.[26]

19. "Macpherson's Lament"

Fare-well, ye dun-geons dark & strong, The wretch's des-tin - ie! Mc -

Pher-son's time will not be long On___ yon-der___ gal - lows tree. Sae

rant-ing-ly, sae wan-ton-ly, Sae daunt-ing-ly gaed he, ___ He

play'd a spring and danc'd it___round Be - low the___gal - lows tree.

Source: The Scots Musical Museum, vol. 2 (Edinburgh: Johnson, 1788), no. 114. This tune is given here as it appeared in a revised edition by William Stenhouse (Edinburgh: Blackwood, 1853), p. 117.

"A particular favorite of his lordship's" was the song "Says Celia to a Reverend Dean," which Charles Cole sang on June 4, 1751, along with several other unspecified songs.[27]

20. "Says Celia to a Reverend Dean"

Says Celia to a Rev'rend Dean,
What reason can be given,
Since marriage is a holy thing
That there are none in heaven?
There are no Women there, he said,
But she replied in Jest,
Women there are, but I'm afraid,
They cannot find a Priest.

Source: The text is in Hamilton, "History" 2 : 403. No other sources are known to exist.

William Lux, the club's only keyboard performer, first appeared as a composer and singer of the song "Let Sots Implore the God of Wine" on November 26, 1751. The following passage documents another instance of fitting an existing melody to a newly composed text: "A gentleman invited to the club, according to ancient custom, vizt. Crinkum Crankum Esqr. [William Lux], afterwards a longstanding member, proposed the singing of a new song, which he himself had composed, in praise of his Lordship and the club, and leave being granted him to sing it, he performed it to the tune of Come Jolly Bacchus &ct. the Secretary accompanying his voice, con violoncello solo."[28] "Come Jolly Bacchus" was a very popular tune and can be found in several eighteenth-century collections and ballad operas, notably *The Devil to Pay*, performed in Annapolis in 1752.

21. "Let Sots Implore the God of Wine"

Let sots im-plore the God of Wine to crown their hours with plea - -
Let Col-ley vain-ly _ court the nine, to ham-mer out his _ mea - -
sure
sure   My muse in-vites each jo-vial soul To find the _

depths of _ glass _ and _ bowl _ In pled-ging round the _ no - ble
Jole the foun - tain of our _ plea - - sure.

See! Honor flashes from his eyes,
at every noble story,
See! Fame exalts him to the skies,
and records probe his glory.

In majesty rever'd, he sits,
and frowns, and smiles, and laughs by fits,
and curbs the pride of wicked wits
That would eclipse his glory.

No more let grand Hugh pretend
to war with Jole's own thunder
but humbly beg, and lowly bend,
the table to knock under,

For like La Mancha's glorious knight
our heroe vanquishes in fight
and never yet was put to flight
To everybody's wonder.

Let sullen mortals hub their spleen
and misers hoard their treasure,
Let debauchers and brothels glean
and then repent at Leisure.

While we enjoy the circling glass
and laugh, and sing, and toast our lass,
We care not who's the sneering ass
That would destroy our pleasure.

Envy may grin a ghastly smile,
Ill nature may revile us,
Folly pretend to make a coil,
or Scandal to defile us.

But while the heart of Jole holds stout,
and all our punch and wine is out
with double strength we'll put to rout,
Those foes that wish to foil us.

Longstanding members, great and small
Who truely know this treasure,
Sing in the chorus, one and all
Continuance to your pleasure,

The Bumper fill, hand round the bowl,
Show you've a true and loyal soul
And pledge the health of Noble Jole,
The Stay of all your pleasure—

Source: The tune was copied from Charles Coffey's *Devil to Pay* (London: Watts, 1748), p. 4, where it is identified as "Air II. Charles of Sweden." The text is recorded as it appears in Hamilton, "History" 2:453–54.

At sederunt 172 it was ordered that Jonas Green prepare a song for the next meeting, to be sung to "some lamentable old tune," mourning the absence of their president, Charles Cole.[29] Green produced the song "O! What's Become of Noble Jole" for the meeting of February 4, 1752: "This piece was played and sung in Club, to the ancient mournful tune of Chevy Chace, con voce, violino & violoncello solo, Crinkum Crankum Esqr. [William Lux], performing the vocal part, Philo Dogmaticus Esqr. [Alexander Malcolm], the violino part & Mr. Secretary [Hamilton] the violoncello."[30]

22. "O! What's Become of Noble Jole"

Rhime In vain, the sing-ers go be-fore, and
CH: O Jole! Jole! Jole! where art thou Jole! where

min-strells come be-hind, In vain on Jole's known
art thou gone a-way, O lam-men-ta-ble

name we call, No Jole, a-las, we find.
and for-sooth, A-lake and wail a day.

The birds lament the general loss,
The beasts in concert groan.
The little fish pop up their heads
and cry, alas! he's gone.
oft when with beating breasts we cry,
O Jole, where art thou, where,
Echo, from each resounding hill
Replies he is not here

Chorus: O Jole! etc.

Lo, here's thy valiant knight, Sir John,
In quarrels brisk and warm.
with sword and pistol, pike and gun,
To guard thee from all harm.
The chancellor does likewise bend
all on his knee so low
To render back the ill got seal,
and be no more thy foe

Chorus: O Jole! etc.

Then here's thy faithful orator
with folio book in hand,

well skill'd in learned eloquence
To wait thy high command.
And here is eke thy Laureat
Who pen'd this goodly verse,
and here is Proto Musicus
Who does these lines rehearse

Chorus: O Jole! etc.

With each longstanding member round
all at this dead of night
Hoping they wish, & wishing hope
of Jole to have a sight
Singing they weep, and weeping Sing,
The loss of Jole away
O Lamentable, and forsooth!
Alake! and wail a day!

Chorus: O Jole! etc.

Source: The text is from Hamilton, "History" 2:510–12; the tune can be located in *A Second Set of Scots Songs* (Edinburgh: Bremner, [1757]), p. 28. Claude Simpson, *The British Broadside Ballad and Its Music* (New Brunswick: Rutgers University Press, 1966), pp. 96–101, describes three eighteenth-century tunes known by the title "Chevy Chace." Bremner's tune appears in his collection compiled for Allan Ramsay's poetry, a collection whose melodies were probably drawn from sources familiar to the Tuesday Club Scots. Furthermore, this tune simply fits the text better than the other two. Nevertheless, the remaining melodies cannot be ruled out. The version known as "Flying Fame" (Simpson, *British Broadside Ballad*, p. 97) is certainly mournful, but its Dorian melody and modal Scots rhythm are very unlike the club's other songs, and the lively meter of the third tune (Simpson, *British Broadside Ballad*, p. 98) appears to contradict Green's poetry.

At a very musical meeting on October 26, 1752, John Lomas sang several favorite songs, including "She Tells Me, with Claret" and "Bumpers Squire Jones," and Jonas Green entertained the members with an "Old Club Song of Robin and Jeck." The poet laureate not only sang this song but also played it on his French horn.[31]

23. "Robin & Jeck"

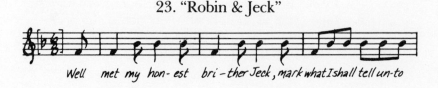

Well met my hon-est bri-ther Jeck, mark what I shall tell un-to

thee, My moth-er tells me that I do lack a wo-man to wait up-on me, She tells me that I must get me a wife, and all— to change a bat-che-lor's life, which makes me a-fraid of great care and strife, Oh chan-ges, fam-i-ly chan-ges, makes me a-fraid to wed.

Jeck:
'Tis like you are afraid to wed
Because the times are hard,
But put such thoughts out of your head
And do not such things regard
For if you can get money, when times are so dear,
Oh! then Brother Robin'ill make it appear.
In times of great plenty, much money you'll clear,
Oh! marry pray thee then marry. Joan's a pritty girl.

Robin:
I do not know whether honest Joan,
Will marry with me, I declare
For she to such a height is grown,
That if I by chance come there
And offer to kiss her, she turns her about,
And with her bold fist she batters my snout,
The blood at the same runs trickling out,
O Marry! if I should marry,
how would she serve me then?

Jeck:
'Tis like you did not compliment,
and give her a kind embrace,
but like some country booby you went,
with your hat flapp'd over your face
It may be, your stockings and shoes were untied,
Like some country booby you lack at the bride
For some such thing she licked your hide,
O Robin! Honest Sweet Robin,
is it the truth or no?

Robin:
I do declare, as I'm a man
True breeding I did express,
And, as you know, I very well can,
I went in a handsome dress.
With my grandfather's hat & my calf leather cloaths
And into her presence I merrily goes,
And made her a compliment down to her toes
But Joan, angry Joan,
she kick'd me about the room.

Jeck:
You should have told her what you had,
To bring a young woman unto
Which would have made her heart full glad,
Without any more to do.
You should have told her "If you will be mine,
all the young turkies, and capons and swine,
and everything else in the world shall be thine,"
Oh Robin! honest sweet Robin,
you would have gain'd her love.

Go try your fortune once again
and be not daunted so
But be resolved to hold out,
For lasses are coy, you know
Tell her, "Love is a thing that can't be conceal'd,"
And be resolved, not for to yield,
And you shall be heir of a conquer'd field
Oh Robin! Play thy way, Robin,
She will at last be thine.

Robin:
I'll try my fortune once again,
I'll court this young damsel once more
I'll give her custard, cakes and wine,
Which I never did before.
I'll spend a round shilling, then when I have done,
I'll call her base slut, and away I will run,
Oh leave her! Utterly leave her,
never come to her no more.

Source: Hamilton, "History" 3:280–82. No other source is known to exist. "Robin & Jeck" is probably a round, although a clumsy one. It can be sung in three parts with the addition of a four-measure rest at the conclusion of the song.

Several pieces of music were played by the club's instrumentalists at
sederunt 188 (October 26, 1752), including two songs by Henry Purcell,
originally written for the play *Bonduca* in 1695. These songs, "To Arms"
and "Britains Strike Home," were often published as a pair and were included in such collections as *Orpheus Britannicus* of 1721 and *The Musical
Entertainer* of 1737 (see source note following song 25).

24. "To Arms"

[8] cess de-pends up-on our Hearts and Spears; the O - ra-cle for

cess de-pends up-on our Hearts and Spears; the O - ra-cle for

[8] War_____ de-clare, for War_____ de-clares, suc-

War_____ de-clare, for War_____ de-clares, suc-

[8] cess de-pends, suc-cess de-pends up - on our_ Hearts and Spears. _____

cess de-pends, suc-cess de-pends up - on our Hearts and Spears. _____

25. "Britains Strike Home"

[8] Bri -tains strike home, re - venge, _ re - venge _ your Coun - try's

Bri -tains strike home, re - venge, _ re - venge your Coun — try's

[8] wrongs:_____ Fight,   Fight and re - cord,   Fight,

wrongs:_____ Fight,   Fight and re - cord,   Fight,

Source: Orpheus Britannicus: A Collection of all the Choicest Songs Compos'd by Mr. Henry Purcell, 3d ed. (1721; rpt., Ridgewood, N.J.: Gregg Press, 1965), pp. 74–76. See also *The Musical Entertainer*, vol. 2 (London: Corbett, [1737]), pp. 97–98. Both songs were printed on three staves in *Orpheus*; in order to save space, I have deleted the lower part of song 24, because it duplicated the lower vocal line except for occasional octave doubling, indicated by brackets. The Tuesday Club instrumentalists probably performed these songs with their standard ensemble, i.e., two violins and cello, the second violin playing the lower vocal line one octave higher.

A Scottish song whose dialect was incomprehensible even to the Tuesday Club Scots was entitled "Newgate Bird Song." It was presented by John

Wollaston, the famous painter, on April 17, 1753. Hamilton recorded the words phonetically and apologized for his rendering of the text, claiming that he was tired: "This old song seemed to excite a little spirit of Gelasticism in the members, tho' they understood nothing at all of the language or dialect in which it was wrote, but the Secretary produced it a little too late, vizt. at eleven a Clock at night, when all the Longstanding members were in a yawning disposition."[32]

26a. "Newgate Bird Song"

As I der-rik'd a-long to dorse on my kin, young Pol-ly the froe-ful I

trout-ed   She nail-ed a cull of his tel-ter and nob, but in

foil-ing his lal-ter was rout-ed.   As I haik-ed a-long __ she

grap-pled my shell She tipt me young boe-man, I know her full well The

har-man spik'd af-ter, but dam'him to hell, __ I plumpt him, & saved her from lim-bo.

The Busnapper' kinking, my mopus did seize,
But my right and left daddle I tipt him,
I darken'd his daylights & sow'd up his sees,
And I up, with my dew beaters tript him
Whilst I milled his muzzard, she nubbled his pole,
She haid'd away singing, I pick'd after moll,
She nail'd the Rum Codger, I mill'd the queer Cull,
And away she haik'd to the Cows bowsing.
Whilst snub in the kin, we sat, shining our gobs,
She tipt me the gum very cleanly,
I swear it will never be out of my nob,
The brimstone, she wheedled so beenly.
Round Scrag, her dear daddles, she loving did fold
I tipt her the velvet, her daylights she roll'd,
I love you, said she, for your quiddish and bold
And will dorse with my Jamie till Jamin.

Dear Molly says I, I'll dorse in your hin,
I'm a boeman will never deceive you,
I'll cut a been weed, to keep you in screen,
And rumbling will pad to relieve you,
Your Darbys I dread not, death's common to all
Your riders and rumblers that pad in the mal
I'll shiver my trotters, at fam'd bilboe's ball
And go off like a boeman, that's quiddish.

Source: The text is from Hamilton, "History" 3 : 198–99; the tune, from *The Muses Delight* (Liverpool: Sadler, 1754), p. 178.

"Newgate Bird Song" is entitled "A Cant Song" in *The Muses Delight*, wherein the text sheds some light on Hamilton's rendering by its annotations, which clarify some of the obscure terms.

26b. "A Cant Song"
"The Words by Mr. Stevens"

As I derrick'd along to doss on my pad,
young Molly ye frofile I touted;
She'd nail'd a rum codger of tilter and nab,[a]
But in filing his tatler[b] was routed:
As I trolled[c] along I grappl'd[d] her shell,
She stag'd ye rum bowman & knew me full well,

ye harmans tap'd her but d——me to hell,
I plumpt'm & sav'd 'er fro limbo.

The buznapper's[e] kenchin my rummer did seize,
But I soon right and left daddle tipt him;
I darken'd his daylights, and sew'd up his sees,
And up with my dew-beaters[f] tript him:
While I mill'd his mazzard she snaffl'd his poll,[g]
Away she went laughing, I hik'd after Moll;
We fil'd the rum codger and plumpt the queer cull,
And away we went to the ken boozie.[h]

As there we sat yaffling[i] and sluicing our gobbs,
She tipt me the gum very cleanly;
L——d d——me 'twill never be out of my nob,
The brimstone she wheedled so bienly;
Round my scrag her dear daddles did lovingly fold,
She tipt me the velvet, her daylights she roll'd;
She said I must love you, you're quiddish and bold,
You shall doss with me Jemmy till jamming.[j]

Dear Molly, he cried, I will doss in your pad,
I'm a bowman that ne'er will deceive you;
I'll cut a bien wid for to keep you in scran,
And boldly will pad to relieve you:
The darbies[k] I dread not, death's common to all,
Those that rumble in rattlers[l] or pad in the Mall;
I can but shake trotters at fam'd Bilby's ball[m]
And go off like a bowman that's quiddish.

[a] tilter and nab: sword and hat
[b] tatler: watch
[c] trolled: loiter'd
[d] grappl'd: took hold of her
[e] buznapper's kenchin: constable's assistant
[f] dew-beaters: feet
[g] snaffl'd his poll: stole his wig
[h] ken boozie: alehouse
[i] yaffling and sluicing: eating and drinking
[j] jamming: hanging
[k] darbies: fetters
[l] rattlers: coaches
[m] Bilby's ball: gallows

Source: The Muses Delight (Liverpool: Sadler, 1754), p. 178.

————————

Charles Cole composed the melody for a poem by Jonas Green, concerning a mock trial, and sang the song at a meeting held on February 25, 1755. With the exception of the anniversary odes, it is the only song completely composed by club members. This is Hamilton's introduction to the song: "This poem being read in Club, his honor the president took the paper in his hand, and gravely putting on his spectacles, sung it to an excellent new Tune of his own setting with a proper chorus, Jonathan Grog Esqr. [Jonas Green], standing bolt upright by the chair, to join his honor in the chorus according to his sentence, in which chorus also, the whole Club joined in the manner following."[33]

27. "The Jurors for the City Bring"

Confesses that when them he bought
he ne'er imagin'd to do nought,
For that the man, Shafter by name,
From whom 'tis clear he bought the same
Did bring them to his house, and there
The said Shafter show'd the pair
and said the pumps did not fit him
They were too wide, or else too slim,
and he would change them if King pleas'd
But King not liking to be teiz'd,
Made him an offer of a crown,
Instead of changing, tho' 'tis known,
a pair of pumps, if good for ought,
are worth two crowns as well as groat,
For which King sold them, that is clear,
Nay, his own oath mades it appear,
Now what said honest Jurors think
Is that said Thomas ought to stink.
For the said King might well conceive
That Shafter the said pumps did thieve

or else so cheap, he would not sell
and that said King must know full well
The whole of this, we now submit,
For you to do as you think fit.

Source: Hamilton, "History" 3:548–50. This portion of the history is in the Maryland Historical Society's Dulany Papers, MS. 1265. See also Breslaw, ed., *Records*, sederunt 237, Feb. 25, 1755. Presumably, the chorus should be repeated following every fourth line.

––––––––––

The final song recorded in the Tuesday Club documents is one played by Charles Love, one of Maryland's few professional musicians of that time (see chap. 3). It was called "The Quaker Sermon" and was performed at the club's tenth anniversary, observed on May 27, 1755.[34]

28. "The Quaker Sermon"

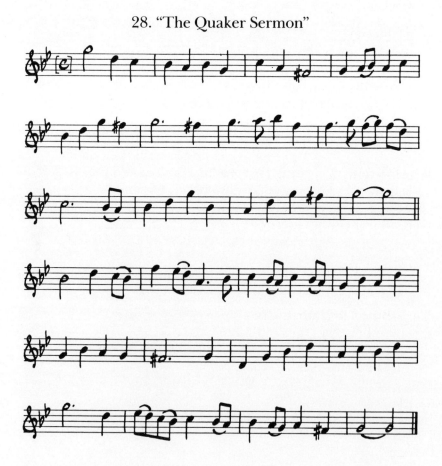

In Playford's *Dancing Master* this tune is accompanied by a song text as well as by dance instructions, as follows:

[Instruction]
First all joyn Hand in Hand, and Face to the Presence, then all lead to the Presence and back again.

> [Song]
> Friends each with Sister, thus in order stand,
> For sure the Godly, may joyn hand in hand;
> In Vertue's Paths tread, firm as Oaks do grow,
> But from all sin, like *Crabs* let's backward go.

[Instruction]
Here the first two couple give Right Hands, and take Left a whole round; next men and we. Facing each other, the two first couple Nod Heads at each other and afterwards take Hands, then all four go once round, and the first couple cast off below the second couple.

> [Song]
> Joyn not with those, who ha'n't the light within,
> Who are in darkness, and in deadly sin;
> But with thy Holy Brethren, joyn thy might,
> Who have like us, the Sanctifyed light?
>
> And tho' we'll not Clap hands, nor Congies make,
> Yet we'll Nod Heads, and Hands we'll Friendly shake;

[Instruction]
Then each Friend standing opposite to his Sister; after he has repeated these two Verses, he Kisses her; Then turning to the second woman, having repeated these Verses Kisses her also.

> [Song]
> Which done, thus joyn'd in Love once round we'll go,
> Next, ye walk up, and we'll cast off below.
>
> But as this Mirth, does much my Spirit move,
> So I to thee, thus testifye my Love;
> And least, O! Sister, thou should'st take this ill,
> The Spirit bears to thee, the same good will.

Source: John Playford, *The Dancing Master*, 4th ed., vol. 2 (London: Young, 1728), pp. 52–53. No fiddle tune or song of this title has come to light, although *The National Tune Index* (text index) lists nineteen titles beginning with the word "Quaker." The tune recorded

here is titled "The Quakers Dance" in Young's edition of Playford's collection; it was selected because the melody is accompanied by a song text that appears to be a sermon in
verse.

Thomas Bacon's catch "See, See, My Boys" is not mentioned in Tuesday
Club documents; it is included here because it was composed by a club
member and was therefore probably sung in Maryland.

29. "See, See, My Boys"

Source: The Gentleman's Catch Book (Dublin: Mountain, [1786]), p. 25.

The titles above do not constitute a complete list of songs played or sung in the Tuesday Club; they are simply the only pieces identified by title, text, or tune. Many were club favorites and were often performed. Only their first appearance in club documents is noted in this text. Both the history and the records contain many additional accounts of music performed in the club for which neither composer nor composition is noted. This additional repertoire must remain a matter of informed conjecture (see chap. 3).

The importance of Tuesday Club songs and instrumental music is vividly conveyed by Hamilton's detailed description of a "Grand Musical Entertainment" performed by Bacon and others on October 26, 1752:

At Sederunt 188, Tunebelly Bowser Esqr. [Richard Dorsey], being H.S. [honorable steward, or host] The orator pronounced a panegyric on Laconic Comus Esqr. [John Lomas], who was entertained as a stranger at this sederunt, pursuant to ancient custom and wished him in the name of his honor the president and the club, a good voyage to England, he Intending soon to take his departure, which done, Mr. Comus rose up, returned the Secretary a Low bow, and sitting down again, sung the two favorite airs of She Tells me with Claret &ct. and Bumpers Squire Jones with great mirth and glee. At Supper, the Secretary, who had a foolish sort of a genius for drawing, took his honor's portrait upon a blank leaf of the Club Record book, with a black lead pencil which hit the likeness so exactly that the Longstanding members approved much of the execution and, the portraits of Sir John, the Chancellor, and the rest of the Longstanding Members were afterwards taken in the same manner, and placed at the beginning of the record book, tho' none but his honor's was finished at this sederunt.

Thus did this diligent and industrious officer, do all in his power, merely ex officio, that is, without fee or reward, to Eternise the memory of this ancient and honorable Club, both by his pencil and pen, for soon after this he began to collect and compile the History of the Club.

Jonathan Grog Esqr. [Green], after supper, sung with great vivacity and humor, the old Club ditty of Robin and Jeck, and afterwards played it upon the french horn, to the great solace and satisfaction of the whole club.

Signior Lardini [Thomas Bacon] and the grand band of Instrumental music, Played To Arms, and Britons Strike Home, and then the Club music, with three violins, a violoncello, french horn and drum, the Grand Chorus was nobly performed, all the voices in the Room Joining in the Concert, and many loud huzzas were given, and many hearty and loyal healths were drank, to his honor Mr. President Jole, which drew about the house a vast number of auditors and spectators, both black and white, the weather being hot, and the window sashes of the Club room drawn up.

After which the whole Company adjourned down to Mr. Leidermonts [Samuel Middleton], a tavern at the Dock, having first sung some merry catches, and then marched thro' the street in good order, with colors flying, drums beating and the french horn a sounding the grand club march against Sir Hugh Maccarty Esqr., his honor walking in great state, at the head of

the procession, and, being arrived at the dock, amidst the confused noise of dogs and children, they routed Mr. Protomusicus
Neverout [William Thornton] out of bed, to which he had retired, being fatigued that night by dancing with the ladies at the
state house, they spent several merry hours, in performing of
vocal and Instrumental music, celebrating his honor and the
club, and drinking good Rack punch and Claret, which his
honor the president, graciously and generously made to flow
like an exuberant fountain, but as the clubical frolic, is best described, in an excellent Heroic Poem to my readers, as being a
piece of admirable Ingenuity, and highly worthy of their pe-
rusal, the piece follows.[35]

Subdivided into three cantos, the lengthy "Heroic Poem" of over 500
lines contains several obscure references to other songs and alludes to the
club instrumentalists playing from books of "Corelli, Vivaldi, Alberti, and
others." This must have been quite a festive evening. Green recorded that
the debris from the party included thirteen quart bottles that "lay dead
on the floor, and nine gallon bowls had been emptied, and more." One
member departed via a window, and the poor innkeeper, Samuel Middleton, passed out shortly before dawn.[36] The tavern proved more durable
than its owner; to this day it stands and serves its customers on the city
dock in Annapolis.

Odes and Incidental Music

The most remarkable musical compositions in the annals of colonial Annapolis were the anniversary odes and incidental music of the Tuesday
Club, a modern edition of which is presented in Part II of this book. Only
three of Jonas Green's odes were set to music: those of the fifth, sixth, and
eighth anniversaries, for the years 1750, 1751, and 1753. A few additional pieces and an overture for the 1752 ode (which was never set to
music) were included with the 1751 and 1753 odes, and a "Minuet for His
Honor," which concluded the seventh anniversary in 1752, appears separately in the Tuesday Club documents.[37] The aforementioned music is all
included in Hamilton's history of the Tuesday Club. The club's records
also contain the overture to the 1750 ode, the entire ode of 1751, and
some of the club's incidental music. The music manuscripts in the history
were themselves probably never used for performances, since all the musical odes were written before 1754 when Hamilton began writing his account. Consequently, wrong notes and other obvious copying errors were
not corrected, as they might have been had the music actually been performed from these manuscripts. The music bound with the records may

also have been copied from earlier versions; the manuscript paper is of an unusual size, matching that of Hamilton's fair copy, a possible indication that this music was set down over a relatively brief span of time, specifically for inclusion in the records. But the worn condition of the manuscript compared with the records and its inclusion as an unpaginated appendix suggest that this was a working copy probably used by club musicians. It is certainly the older of the two versions and may even be Bacon's original score. From one of Hamilton's drawings, it is clear that the instrumentalists read from parts rather than from full score,[38] but these parts have been lost.

The three odes represent the work of several club composers and display many similarities. The texts were composed by Green. His poetical style is consistent, as is his dramatic structure—alternating recitatives, arias, and unison choruses. The choruses, in general, are rhythmically and melodically simpler than the arias and are written in a more easily singable range, which suggests that most choruses were intended to be sung by the entire club. The texture of both the odes and incidental music is usually three-part, scored for two violins and cello. The vocal line is always one of the treble parts and would probably have been doubled by a violin. Secco recitatives are accompanied by an unfigured bass line. There are other occasional two-part sections in both instrumental and vocal passages and a single virtuoso movement for unaccompanied cello in the ode of 1753.

Thomas Bacon wrote overtures for the 1750, 1751, and 1752 odes. The 1753 overture and ode were composed by "several hands," not including Bacon (see p. 47). Evidence suggests that it is probably the product of a collaboration by Hamilton and Malcolm. Hamilton had written the 1750 ode, except for the overture, and Malcolm certainly understood the general harmonic and contrapuntal practices of the early eighteenth century. His treatise did not include a study of musical form; similarly, Hamilton's music of the 1750 ode reveals a lack of formal organization, which could account for some of the unusual compositional practices found in the ode of 1753.

Bacon's 1750 overture consists of a slow opening movement with the character of a French overture, followed by three contrasting dances: a gavotte, minuet, and pastorale.[39] All are in the key of A major and are in binary form, with first sections ending on a dominant cadence. Repeats are not consistently indicated, but both sections of these binary dance movements should probably be repeated. There are a few abrupt harmonic shifts such as the modulation from the dominant to the relative minor in measures 9–13 (ex. 1), and the treatment of dissonance is sometimes unusual, in that both the dissonant tone and its resolution are sounded together (ex. 2).

Example 1. Thomas Bacon, Overture to the Anniversary Ode of 1750, 1st movement (Adagio), mm. 10–13.

Example 2. Thomas Bacon, Overture to the Anniversary Ode of 1750, 4th movement (Pastorale), m. 56.

Voice leading is not always smooth, but melodies seem well thought-out, emanating from an opening motive in typical baroque fashion. There is no development, and the use of melodic sequence is minimal, usually limited to single repetitions of short melodic passages, such as the modulation from the relative minor to the tonic, illustrated in example 3.

The 1751 overture opens with a seven-measure largo, followed by an aria and a gavotte, both in binary form.[40] In these pieces Bacon's harmonic organization is always clear; each movement is in G major, with dominant cadences concluding each opening section, invariably followed by a modulation to the relative minor in the second portion of these two-part forms. As seen in his gavotte (ex. 4), Bacon understood the use of dominant pedal points to heighten harmonic tension before final cadences. In general, he stayed well within the conventions of eighteenth-century composition and must be regarded as a skilled, if not masterful, composer.

Example 3. Thomas Bacon, Overture to the Anniversary Ode of 1750,
1st movement (Adagio), mm. 17–20.

Example 4. Thomas Bacon, Overture to the Anniversary Ode of 1751,
3d movement (Gavotte), mm. 60–63.

The 1753 overture differs in several respects: three of its pieces are
in different keys and are scored for varying combinations of instruments.[41] Sequences are extensively employed, and the harmonic sense
of direction evident in the earlier overtures appears weaker in this work.
In the gavotte melodic passages occur in uncharacteristically irregular
lengths. The composers solved this short-phrase problem by abbreviating
measure 40 (ex. 5). Consecutive fifths and octaves, incomplete harmonies, awkward leaps, and odd voice leadings are not unusual. The solo
cello section has no apparent organization but is simply a series of melodic fragments, presented in sequences interspersed with cadential for-
mulas. In short, the 1753 overture appears to be the work of musicians
who knew how music should sound but not how to organize their musical
materials effectively.

Example 5. Anonymous, Overture to the Anniversary Ode of 1753, 3d movement (Gavotta Grande), mm. 36–37, 40.

Each of the three odes is distinctly different. Hamilton's 1750 ode is a thirteen-movement work that displays strong melodic lines but reveals the composer's failure to understand traditional harmonic organization.[42] His constant chromatic alteration of diatonic chords produced chains of secondary dominants that carried him away from the tonic, and he often made no attempt to return to it. His opening recitative, "Thrice Hail Serene Returning Day" (see Part II), begins in A minor and finishes in G major; the following aria commences in B minor and ends in D major, and the ensuing chorus, "Fortune Ever Changing," begins in F major and closes in A minor. This modulation to the mediant, although common, is not consistent. The fourth piece, a recitative, "Honor & Justice," opens in A major and ends in D minor, and the succeeding aria, "Should Any Bold Intruder Dare," is the composer's first piece to begin and end in the same key, thanks to its da capo ritornello. The next chorus, "Till Bruis'd to Mash, & Crushed to Powder," again shows Hamilton's tendency to move to the mediant, from G major to B minor. Following this B-minor cadence, Hamilton jolts his audience with a recitative, "High in the Chair," which opens in F major but cadences in G major. The remainder of the ode is predominately in D major, commencing with the aria "Apollo with His Band of Singers," an adaptation of Thomas Arne's "Serenade," written for the Drury Lane Theater's *Merchant of Venice*. The aria "Let This Glad Evening Crown the Day" is in G major and, despite a modulation to the dominant, returns to the tonic via an unlikely succession of chords, although it drifts finally to B minor. This particular aria does achieve a degree of formal coherence through the repetition of an instrumental ritornello, which appears first in the tonic, later in the dominant, and then returns to the tonic. The final "Grand Chorus" displays Hamilton's grasp of a style that might be termed "stately British" and is followed by a "Symphonia" whose melody echoes an accompanying figure from the preceding chorus. Both pieces are, surprisingly, in D major.

The individual movements of the ode are, for the most part, through-composed, the only structural repetitions being the aforementioned ritornelli; the eighteenth-century counterpoint is nonimitative and generally correct. The ode is scored in three parts, except for the recitatives, two arias ("Till Bruis'd" and "Apollo"), and one chorus ("The Canopy"), which are all written in two parts. Hamilton's melodies are usually interesting, often expressive, and well formed. He knew how to strengthen a

Example 6. Alexander Hamilton, Anniversary Ode of 1750, chorus, "Till Bruis'd," mm. 191–97.

Example 7. Alexander Hamilton, Anniversary Ode of 1750, aria, "Airy Violins," mm. 96–99.

Example 8. Alexander Hamilton, Anniversary Ode for 1750, chorus, "While Jole Shall Live," vocal line, mm. 356–62.

cadence by using repetition and increasing rhythmic activity (ex. 6), and he employed word painting with good effect in such passages as "Apollo heightens our delight" (ex. 7) and the extended melisma on "Joy" (ex. 8).

There is an element of mystery concerning the 1750 ode. The description of the fifth anniversary in the history notes: "After supper, the musicians con stromenti of the Club, played the overture of the anniversary music, with two violins and a bass. . . . Solo Neverout Esqr. [Thornton], Protomusicus con voce, did not perform the canto part of the music this night, not being sufficiently prepared."[43] Evidently the music to the ode existed at the anniversary celebration, but there is no evidence that it was ever performed. A letter, entered in the records, suggests that Bacon, not Hamilton, wrote the music for this ode; the secretary enclosed the ode in a letter to Anthony Bacon, hoping that it might be published in the *Gentleman's Magazine*: "I have sent you enclosed this ode, and would also have sent you the music set to it by your brother, in three parts, but it would have made the package too bulky."[44] Thomas Bacon may have assisted Hamilton, but stylistic differences between this work and Bacon's 1751 ode are so striking that the inscription "Music by Signior Secretario" (i.e., Hamilton), which appears below the overture at the beginning of the ode, must be taken at face value. Hamilton's work was probably played, since corrections to his manuscript show that someone attempted to make musical sense out of some of the stranger passages.

Bacon's 1751 ode was the club's favorite.[45] It was publicly performed in the Annapolis council chamber, and its most popular sections were often heard in club meetings.[46] The ode consists of an overture and eight movements and is musically much more coherent than Hamilton's setting of the 1750 ode. Bacon's composition is solidly in G major until the G minor chorus "Ah! Noble Cole" (see Part II). Then comes a recitative, "Ye Muses Nine," which begins in D major and moves to E minor, leading into an extended A-major aria, "As When the Morning Chases Night." The final movements—arias, march, and chorus—are all in D major.

Bacon's work displays considerable structural skill. His arias are extended pieces featuring contrasting sections. The opening aria, "Io, Io, Io, with Triumphant Noise," begins with a lively fifteen-measure introduction that concludes with a strong drive to a tonic cadence, followed by two repeated sections, the first of which is thematically related to the introduction. This first portion of the aria ends with a two-measure instrumental flourish reminiscent of the introduction. The next part of the aria, "No gloomy thought," is of a contrasting character: written in 3/8, this binary section is more lyrical and more chromatic, cadencing in E minor before returning to G major and featuring an obvious example of word painting with its diatonic runs on "but merry, merry, merry." The short chorus "Ah! Noble Jole" is also in binary form, with an instrumental coda. This unison chorus, in 12/8, has the character of an Irish jig.

The second aria, "As When the Morning Chases Night," is a minuet-aria in ternary form, without indicated repeats. The piece opens with an instrumental introduction that presents the theme of the first vocal section; the three divisions are not otherwise thematically related. Following the third section is a brief, written-out vocal cadenza, with a series of rests preceding the cadence, thereby inviting further improvisation; the piece concludes with a four-measure instrumental coda in common time.

Bacon continued the ode with another aria rather than a chorus, as specified by Green.[47] Composed in D major, this lyrical piece can be performed as an extension of the previous aria. Its simple melody (reminiscent of the old Shaker tune "Simple Gifts") contrasts with the preceding aria's florid passages. Bacon's "Club March against Sir Hugh Mccarty" (purported president of a rival New York club) is a model eighteenth-century march in the tradition of Jeremiah Clark, John Stanley, and George Frideric Handel. It is in binary form, with a final phrase that repeats the closing measures of the first section. Bacon inserted this march; it was not part of Green's ode. The final chorus, "Long Live Illustrious Cole," a ternary piece with no thematic repetition, was a particular favorite of the Tuesday Club and was usually performed by all its members.

The scoring of the 1751 ode is in three parts, excepting recitatives and occasional instrumental passages. Its counterpoint is nonimitative and follows the common practice of eighteenth-century composition. Melodies are well formed and graceful, often extended by sequences, particularly in modulating passages. Bacon's odes incorporate elements of eighteenth-century Italian baroque and British folk music, featuring short instrumental movements reminiscent of Corelli, Irish Jigs, Italian coloratura vocal writing, lyrical English melodies, and country dances, combined with a good measure of appropriate pomposity. His music is eminently performable and is an effective vehicle for Green's entertainingly pompous poetry.

Two incidental pieces, both by Bacon, appear in the Tuesday Club documents along with the 1751 ode. The history and the records include a "Minuet for Sir John," which is also found in the Ormsby manuscript as "A Minuet by the Reverd. Mr. Bacon" (Pt. II, p. 283).[48] The minuet is typical of the period, with the following phrase structure: abac (repeated) deac (repeated). An additional minuet with six variations, "Grand Club Minuet *con variatione*," displaying Bacon's familiarity with variation technique, is found in the history.[49] All its movements are in G major and usually feature one principal instrument with two accompanying voices. In the first variation the first violin has an arpeggiated theme; in variations 2 and 3, leading parts are given to the cello and second violin, respectively, and both lines feature ornamental sixteenth-note passagework. In variation 4, the first violin again is the focus of interest, with its ascending arpeggios. The fifth variation features syncopation in the upper two voices, and triplets permeate the sixth variation in all parts. Harmonic structure is essentially the same in all variations.

The 1753 ode comprises eleven movements, only five of which are vocal pieces.[50] This ode displays neither Hamilton's harmonic meanderings nor Bacon's structural finesse but is nonetheless interesting. D major serves as its ultimate tonal center. After an overture (see Part II) in G major and D major, the opening aria, "Sing Again," in C major, is followed by an F-major chorus, "Come All Ye Fine Fid'lers," which eventually ends in A minor—a modulation that suggests Hamilton may have composed the chorus. A minuet and gavotte, both in D major, follow and are succeeded by a recitative, "In Grand Consistory," that moves from D major to B minor. The jig-aria "Whilst the Valiant Sir John" returns to D major, the key of the final three pieces, "Minuet for Sir John," "March for Sir John," and the concluding "General Grand Chorus," which begins in B minor but modulates to its relative major, ending in D.

Although the instrumental pieces in this ode follow standard forms, the vocal works display a subtler approach to thematic organization. They feature frequent instrumental interludes and vocal lines that expand and repeat melodic fragments, thus lending a thematic unity unlike that of the two earlier odes. Texture, counterpoint, and traditional word-painting devices, on the other hand, resemble the compositional techniques of Hamilton and Bacon.

Several pieces of incidental music appear with the 1753 ode in the history;[51] the first, a "Minuet for the Poet Laureat," is an inept composition, with a second violin part that often doubles either the bass or first violin part, but its melody is not without merit. The composer cannot be positively identified, but the static bass and the alternation between two- and three-part texture is reminiscent of Hamilton. The minuet does not appear to be the work of Bacon, whose skill in writing counterpoint far exceeded that which is evident in this piece. A "Grand Club Jig by Signor Proto musicus," for violin and cello, is in binary form, its melody strong and its rhythm properly exuberant. If William Thornton is, in fact, the composer of this skillful little dance, it is indeed unfortunate that he did not write more music. The attribution in the manuscript is clear; moreover, passages in the Tuesday Club history suggest that Thornton at least tried to play the violin, and he was, after all, the official club musician, albeit "con voce."

The jig is followed by "Overture for His Honor's Entertainment by Signor Lardini," a two-movement work in F major, composed as an overture to the 1752 Anniversary Ode, which was never set to music.[52] The piece opens with a slow movement featuring instrumental flourishes, suggestive of a French overture, and concludes with a gavotte. "Minuet for the Attorney General by Signr. Lardini," in D minor, completes the incidental music bound with the ode of 1753. It is an elegant miniature, whose opening rhythmic pattern, emphasizing the second pulse of the measure, resembles a sarabande.

One additional minuet by Bacon, entitled "Minuet for His Honor," appears separately at the conclusion of Hamilton's description of the seventh anniversary, May 12, 1752.[53] It is a straightforward binary dance in D major, which proceeds conventionally, after an awkward beginning.

The anniversary odes and incidental music in the Tuesday Club manuscripts provide unique insight into the degree of musical sophistication that existed in colonial Maryland during the middle years of the eighteenth century. They represent the principal documentation of an Annapolitan musical taste that complemented its citizens' well-established love of British art and fashion.

NOTES

1. I am indebted to Jonathan Tuck, tutor at St. John's College, Annapolis, for this translation of Hamilton's syntactically problematic Greek quotation.

2. Alexander Hamilton, "The History of the Ancient and Honorable Tuesday Club," 3 vols., The Johns Hopkins University Library and Maryland Historical Society, 3 : 114–16.

3. Ibid. 1 : 143.

4. Ibid., p. 144.

5. Ibid., p. 160. The verse is also given in Robert Chambers, ed., *The Songs of Scotland prior to Burns* (Edinburgh: Chambers, 1862), p. 212.

6. *Musick for Allan Ramsay's Collection of Scots Songs* (Edinburgh: Ramsay, ca. 1726), pp. 116–17; *Calliope; or, English Harmony*, 2 vols. (London: Roberts, 1739–46). The songs were "Auld Rob Morris," "Bumpers Squire Jones," "Orpheus and Euridice," "The Pleasures of Life," "When Cloe We Ply," and "Whilst I Gaze on Chloe, Trembling."

7. *The Musical Miscellany*, vol. 2 (London: Watts, 1729), p. 76.

8. *Maryland Gazette*, July 30, 1752.

9. *The Musical Entertainer*, vol. 1 (London: Bickham, 1737), p. 45.

10. Hamilton, "History" 1 : 162–63. Elaine G. Breslaw, ed., *Records of the Tuesday Club of Annapolis, 1745–56* (Urbana: University of Illinois Press, 1988), sederunt 24, Nov. 12, 1745.

11. Hamilton, "History" 1 : 168; Breslaw, ed., *Records*, sederunt 11, July 23, 1745.

12. J. A. Leo Lemay, *Men of Letters in Colonial Maryland* (Knoxville, University of Tennessee Press, 1972), p. 229, identifies the Baltimore poets as the Reverends Thomas Cradock and Thomas Chase. Their poem, "On the two Miss ******* as they sat before me, hearing of Mr. Whitefield," appears in Hamilton, "History" 1 : 185.

13. "An Infallible Receipt to Cure the Epidemical and Afflecting Distempers of Love and the Poetical Itch," *Maryland Gazette*, Dec. 17, 1745; a receipt for the cure of "Furor Poeticus" and "Febris Amatoria" signed by "Theopholus Polypharmacus, MD" (Hamilton) appeared in the *Gazette* on Feb. 4, 1746; and an advertisement for a runaway servant known as "Bard Bavius" insultingly characterized the Reverend Chase in the *Gazette's* issue of Mar. 18, 1746.

14. Hamilton, "History" 1 : 175–90.

15. Ibid., p. 190, attributes the poem to "the Junto at Batchellor's hall." Hamilton identified the writers of an earlier poem as "Messrs. Blunt [Bullen], Sly [Rev. Gordon], Motely [Marshe], and Scribble [Hamilton]," noting that they met in "Batchellor's Hall" (ibid., p. 186). An additional poet, "Quaint" (Dorsey), is included in ibid., p. 175, with the aforementioned.

16. *Thirty Scots Songs for a Voice and Harpsichord, the Music Taken from the Most Genuine Sets Extant, the Words from Allan Ramsay* (Edinburgh: Robert Bremner, [1757]); Hamilton, "History" 1 : 192–93.

17. Chambers, ed., *The Songs of Scotland prior to Burns*, pp. 196–97; Carolyn Rabson and Kate Van Winkle Keller, *The National Tune Index* (New York: University Music Editions, 1980), text index.

18. Hamilton, "History" 1 : 196.

19. Ibid., p. 281.

20. Ibid., pp. 314–16.

21. Ibid., p. 339.

22. Ibid., p. 374; Breslaw, ed., *Records*, sederunt 193, Nov. 8, 1748.

23. Hamilton, "History" 1 : 423; Breslaw, ed., *Records*, sederunt 102, Mar. 21, 1749.

24. Hamilton, "History" 2 : 114–15. The conundrum in which the question appeared was found on a slip of paper lying on the floor. No one admitted to the composition of the riddle, but Malcolm solved it.

25. Breslaw, ed., *Records*, sederunt 102, Mar. 21, 1749.

26. Hamilton, "History" 2 : 350; Breslaw, ed., *Records*, sederunt 152, Mar. 26, 1751.

27. Hamilton, "History" 2 : 403.

28. Ibid., p. 452; Breslaw, ed., *Records*, sederunt 169, Dec. 10, 1751.

29. Hamilton, "History" 2 : 508; Breslaw, ed., *Records*, sederunt 171, Jan. 7, 1752; sederunt 172, Jan. 21, 1752; and sederunt 173, Feb. 4, 1752.

30. Hamilton, "History" 2 : 512.

31. Ibid. 3:116–18 (for the entire passage, see pp. 108–9); Breslaw, ed., *Records*, sederunt 188, Oct. 26, 1752.

32. Hamilton, "History" 3:200.

33. Ibid., p. 548; Breslaw, ed., *Records*, sederunt 237, Feb. 25, 1755.

34. Breslaw, ed., *Records*, sederunt 240, May 27, 1755.

35. Hamilton, "History" 3:117–19; Breslaw, ed., *Records*, sederunt 188, Oct. 26, 1752.

36. Hamilton, "History" 3:136–38; Breslaw, ed., *Records*, sederunt 188, Oct. 26, 1752.

37. Hamilton, "History" 3:55–56.

38. Ibid. 2, illustration opposite p. 359.

39. Ibid., pp. 147–49; Alexander Hamilton, "Record of the Tuesday Club, Vol. 1," Manuscripts Division, MS. 854, appendix, Maryland Historical Society, Baltimore.

40. Hamilton, "History" 2:371–72; Hamilton, "Record," appendix.

41. Part II, pp. 229–36; Hamilton, "History" 3:218 (1–3). The 1753 ode is separately paginated, beginning at p. 218; numbers in parentheses denote individual pages of this ode.

42. Part II, pp. 150–82; Hamilton, "History" 2:149–62.

43. Hamilton, "History" 2:145; Breslaw, ed., *Records*, sederunt 130, May 15, 1750.

44. Breslaw, ed., *Records*, sederunt 135, July 31, 1750.

45. Part II, pp. 183–216; Hamilton, "History" 2:371–85; Hamilton, "Record," appendix.

46. Hamilton, "History" 2:359 (council chamber); according to the records for May 16, 1751, the ode was repeated two days later in a special club meeting and was revived at the 1752 anniversary celebration, described in the records of May 12, 1752. Portions of this ode, especially the "Grand Chorus," were performed on May 28, 1751, Oct. 26, 1752, and Feb. 6, 1753, according to the entries in the club's minutes for those dates; and Hamilton, "History" 3:117, documents a performance of the entire ode on Oct. 12, 1752. The phrase "club music," which describes the music performed in several meetings, probably refers to the 1751 ode.

47. Hamilton, "History" 2:367. In the text of the ode, Green also indicated that the "Grand Chorus" was originally intended to be a recitative.

48. Ibid., p. 390; Hamilton, "Record," appendix; John Ormsby, manuscript book of minuets (1758), p. 4, Library and Museum of the Performing Arts, Lincoln Center, New York.

49. Part II, pp. 216–24; Hamilton, "History" 2:386–89.

50. Part II, pp. 229–64; Hamilton, "History" 3:218 (1–16).

51. Hamilton, "History" 3:218 (17–22).

52. Breslaw, ed., *Records*, sederunt 205, June 26, 1753.

53. Hamilton, "History" 3:55–56.

6

SUMMARY

Music in colonial Annapolis was an activity of participation rather than observation. Although a few professional musicians were heard, music was, for the most part, an entertainment created by and for amateurs possessing varying skills, representing virtually every social stratum from slave to shopkeeper, from Callister's "wretched fidlers" to Bacon's skilled aristocratic friends. Most of the best musicians were British emigrants; their repertoire encompassed English ballads and Scots songs, and their compositions mimicked European composers whose music was popular in the British Isles—Handel, Corelli, Vivaldi, and their contemporaries.

In the annals of American music, Annapolitan musicians are notable for a number of reasons: in 1752 they evidently participated in the first opera known to have been performed in America with orchestral accompaniment, their public concerts were among the earliest given in the colonies, and their compositions were the first of their genre written in this country.

It is particularly significant that these early compositions were not produced by a single genius, working in a cultural vacuum, but were generated by a whole group of individuals, notably, the Tuesday Club. These gifted amateurs and their friends clearly show that a high level of musical sophistication existed in the American colonies well before the formal establishment of a concert tradition. The various musical abilities and interests of the Tuesday Club aristocrats further demonstrate that appreciation and accomplishment in the fine arts, especially music, was not unusual and that the well-documented musical skill of such colonial leaders as Thomas Jefferson, Benjamin Franklin, and Francis Hopkinson was typical rather than extraordinary.

Why did such a vital organization collapse after ten years of intense activity? Upton Scott, the last surviving member, attributed the club's demise to the death of Hamilton, but it must be noted that dissolution of the club coincided with the gradual dispersal of its musical leadership. Hamilton died in 1756, and Charles Cole, who was also in failing health, died the following year. By that time, however, William Lux had already relocated in Baltimore County, and Thomas Bacon had begun his compilation of the laws of Maryland, before moving to Frederick in 1758. John Lomas returned to England, as did John Wollaston, the artist, and the aging Alexander Malcolm had retired to Queen Anne's County. With Malcolm's departure in July 1754, Hamilton was the only remaining instrumentalist with any real skill, except for Daniel Dulany, Jr., who was an occasional guest. Of the club's most active singers, only Thornton remained, since Charles Cole's health prevented his full participation. Music unquestionably was a primary outlet for the club's creative energies. It is therefore not unreasonable to view the Tuesday Club as one of America's first music societies.

The Tuesday Club is truly a unique organization for the student of colonial culture. Although other musical societies and clubs existed in major colonial cities, their activities are principally known through concert notices and other public records, supplemented by a few entries in private letters and journals. The Tuesday Club documents contain a wealth of information, revealing details of performers and performances, composers and repertoire; most important, those documents, together with this study, provide the music historian with a uniquely intimate view of music in colonial America.

APPENDIX A

Songs from Ballad Operas and Plays
Performed in Annapolis, 1752

I. *The Beggar's Opera*
   John Gay and John Christopher Pepusch (1728)

1. "Through All the Employments of Life"
2. "'Tis Woman That Seduces All Mankind"
3. "If Any Wench Venus' Girdle Wear"
4. "If Love the Virgin's Heart Invade"
5. "A Maid Is Like the Golden Ore"
6. "Virgins Are Like the Fair Flow'r"
7. "Our Polly Is a Sad Slut"
8. "Can Love Be Controlled by Advice"
9. "Oh Polly, You Might Have Toyed and Kissed"
10. "I, Like a Ship in Storms, Was Tossed"
11. "A Fox May Steal Your Hens, Sir"
12. "Oh, Ponder Well! Be Not Severe"
13. "The Turtle Thus with Plaintive Crying"
14. "Pretty Polly, Say, When I Was Away"
15. "My Heart Was So Free, It Roved Like the Bee"
16. "Were I Laid on Greenland's Coast"
17. "Oh What Pain It Is to Part"
18. "The Miser Thus a Shilling Sees"
19. "Fill Ev'ry Glass, for Wine Inspires Us"
20. "Let Us Take the Road"
21. "If the Heart of a Man Is Depressed with Cares"
22. "Youth's the Season Made for Joys"
23. "Before the Barn Door Crowing"
24. "The Gamesters and Lawyers Are Jugglers Alike"
25. "At the Tree I Shall Suffer with Pleasure"
26. "Man May Escape from Rope and Gun"
27. "Thus When a Good Hus-wife Sees a Rat in Her Trap"
28. "How Cruel Are the Traitors Who Lie and Swear"
29. "The First Time at the Looking Glass"
30. "When You Censure the Age"
31. "Is Then His Fate Decreed, Sir"
32. "You'll Think, E'er Many Days Ensue"
33. "If You at an Office So-lic-it Your Due"

34. "Thus When the Swallow, Seeking Prey"
35. "How Happy Could I Be with Either"
36. "I'm Bubbled I'm Bubbled. Oh How I Am Troubled"
37. "Cease Your Funning; Force or Cunning"
38. "Why Now Madam Flirt"
39. "No Pow'r on Earth Can E'er Divide"
40. "I Like the Fox Shall Grieve, Whose Mate Hath Left Her"
41. "When Young at the Bar You First Taught Me to Score"
42. "My Love Is All Maddness and Folly"
43. "Thus Gamesters United in Friendship Are Found"
44. "The Modes of the Court So Common Are Grown"
45. "What Gudgeons Are We Men"
46. "In the Days of My Youth I Could Bill Like Dove"
47. "I'm Like a Skiff on the Ocean Tossed"
48. "When a Wife's in Her Pout (As She's Sometimes, No Doubt)"
49. "A Curse Attends That Woman's Love"
50. "Among the Men, Coquets We Find"
51. "Come, Sweet Lass, Let's Banish Sorrow till Tomorrow"
52. "Hither, Dear Husband, Turn Your Eyes"
53. "Which Way Shall I Turn Me"
54. "When My Hero in Court Appears"
55. "When He Holds Up His Hand Arraigned for His Life"
56. "Ourselves, Like the Great, to Secure a Retreat"
57. "The Charge Is Prepared; the Lawyers Are Met"
58. "Oh Cruel, Cruel, Cruel Case"
59. "Of All the Friends in Time of Grief"
60. "Since I Must Swing, I Scorn"
61. "But Now Again My Spirits Sink"
62. "But Valor the Stronger Grows"
63. "If Thus—a Man Can Die Much Bolder with Brandy"
64. "So I Drink Off This Bumper and Now I Can Stand the Test"
65. "But Can I Leave My Pretty Hussies"
66. "Their Eyes, Their Lips, Their Busses"
67. "Since Laws Were Made for Ev'ry Degree"
68. "Would I Might Be Hang'd and I Would So Too"
69. "Thus I Stand Like the Turk, with His Doxies Around"

II. *Damon and Philida*
   Colley Cibber (1729)

1. "There's Not a Swain"
2. "What Woman Could Do"
3. "Tell Me Philly"
4. "While You Both Pretend"
5. "Away with Suspicion"
6. "While You Pursue Me"
7. "I'll Range the World"
8. "Around the Plains"

9. "A Thousand Ways"
10. "Behold, and See Thy Wounded Lover"
11. "O What a Plague Is Love"
12. "Ah! Poor Cimon! Dud a Cry"
13. "Give Over Your Love, You Great Loobies"
14. "See, Behold, and See"
15. "To the Priest Away"

III. *The Female Parson; or, Beau in the Suds*
    Charles Coffey (1730)

1. "Cupid, Gentle God of Love"
2. "Love Like a Trumpet"
3. "Why Should None Indulge Their Passions"
4. "I Adore Thee, Charming Creature"
5. "Who Can Our Female Arts Withstand"
6. "Happy the Virgin State"
7. "Let Other Maids in Vain"
8. "Plarakanarorka"
9. "As in a Storm at Dead of Night"
10. "Rise Charming Creature"
11. "Prithee, Why So Coy"
12. "If You Would True Courage Show"
13. "My Humor's Frank and Free"
14. "Were Jove's Imperial Crown"
15. "O, How Fine Is a Neat Disguise"
16. "O, Queen of Love"
17. "Thus with Love and Soft Delight"
18. "Whilst Your Eyes"
19. "Thus Laden I Come to Charm Thee"
20. "Thus We Live and We Reign"
21. "I Fly Now on Wings of Desire"
22. "Thus Gay and Airy"
23. "Since Wedlock Is a State in Life"
24. "Long Have I Been with Grief Opprest"
25. "And Now I Am Once More Set Free"
26. "Celia's Eyes Have Lost Their Splendour"
27. "Now We Have Both Been in the Wrong"
28. "Thus Like Happy Turtles Cooing"

IV. *The Devil to Pay; or, The Wives Metamorphos'd*
    Charles Coffey (1731)

1. "He That Has the Best Wife"
2. "'Tis, I Vow and Swear"
3. "Of All the Plagues of Human Life"
4. "Come Jolly Bacchus, God of Wine"
5. "Ye Gods! You Gave to Me a Wife"

6. "Of the States in Life So Various"
7. "Tell Me No More of This, or That"
8. "My Swelling Heart Now Leaps with Joy"
9. "My Little Spirits Now Appear"
10. "Of All the Trades from East to West"
11. "Let Matters of State"
12. "Tho' Late I Was a Cobler's Wife"
13. "Hounds and Horns o'er Plains Resounding"
14. "Fine Ladies with an Artful Grace"
15. "O Charming Cunning Man! Thou Hast Been Wond'rous Kind"
16. "Tho' Ravish'd from My Husband's Arms"
17. "Thus We'll Drown All Melancholy"
18. "Let Every Face with Smiles Appear"

Note: This ballad opera also existed in a full-length version containing forty-two songs. The shortened version was performed as an afterpiece to longer plays; since this was the case with the Annapolis performances, the abbreviated set of eighteen airs is cited here.

V. *An Old Man Taught Wisdom; or, The Virgin Unmask'd*
   Henry Fielding (1735)

1. "Do You, Papa, but Find a Coach"
2. "When He in a Coach Can Be Carry'd"
3. "In Women We Beauty or Wit May Admire"
4. "Ah Be Not Angry, Good Dear Sir"
5. "Ah Sir! I Guess"
6. "The Jokers Have Said, That Men of My Trade"
7. "When Our Wives Deny"
8. "La! What Swinging Lyes Some People Will Tell"
9. "O Press Me Not, Sir, to Be Wife"
10. "When You Are Like Bateman Dead"
11. "What Virgin E'er Wou'd Marry"
12. "I Never Yet Long'd for a Thing in My Life"
13. "Go Marry What Blockhead You Will, Miss"
14. "I Wou'd Have You to Know, You Nasty Thing"
15. "O All Ye Powers Above"
16. "Dearest Charmer"
17. "Excuse Me, Sir; Zounds, What D'ye Mean"
18. "Did Mortal E'er See Two Such Fools"
19. "Oh Dear Papa! Don't Look So Grum"
20. "You May Physick, and Musick, and Dancing Enhance"

VI. Songs from plays

1. "Great Love Inspire Him" (Centilivre, *The Busybody*)
2. "But You Look So Bright" (Farquhar, *The Beaux Stratagem*)
3. "A Trifling Song You Hear" (Farquhar, *The Beaux Stratagem*)
4. "Our Prentice Tom May Now Refuse" (Farquhar, *The Recruiting Officer*)
5. "Come, Fair One, Be Kind" (Farquhar, *The Recruiting Officer*)

6. "But It Is Not So" (Farquhar, *The Recruiting Officer*)
7. "Let Her Wander" (Farquhar, *The Constant Couple*)
8. "Thus Damon Knocked at Celia's Door" (Farquhar, *The Constant Couple*)
9. "And What Shall I Give You" (Farquhar, *The Constant Couple*)
10. "Behold the Goldfinches" (Farquhar, *The Constant Couple*)
11. "No Ice Is So Hard" (Garrick, *Miss in Her Teens*)

Most of the plays call for unspecified music—"enter singing" is a common stage direction. Centilivre's *Busybody* also requires the actors to sing out of tune, dance, and play the spinet.

APPENDIX B

Songs in the *Gentleman's Magazine*, 1744–55

1744

"Blow, Blow, Thou Winter Wind" (Arne)	98
"The Invitation" (anon.)	156
"Tell Me" (Howard)	217
"Cease, Myra" (Stubley)	273
"The Lovers Progress" (Stanley)	390
Melody from *Amorous Goddess* (Howard)	444
Melody from *Amorous Goddess* (Howard)	503
"Bumpers 'Squire Jones" (anon.)	612
"Music and Beauty" (Stanley)	673

1745

"Arno's Vale" (Holcombe)	45
"When Heaves My Fond Bosom" (Howard)	156
"The Shepherd's Invitation" (Lampe)	217
"Idleness" (Boyce)	268
"The Self-banished" (Oswald)	329
"God Save Great George Our King" (anon.)	552
"The Royal Hunter's March" (anon.)	664

1746

"How Faint a Joy" (Allcock)	35
"Spring" (Brerewood)	157
"The Meads and the Groves" (anon.)	269
"The Disappointment" (anon.)	380
"The Ingenuous Lover" (Stubley)	550
"To Flavia" (Allcock)	605

1747

"A Hunting Song" (C. L.)	39
"A Hunting Song" (Ridley) [same text as preceding]	144
"To Celia" (Lord Lansdowne)	392
"O Wouldst Thou Know" (Comte St. Germain)	441
"Command, When Boreas Roughly Blows" (anon.)	489
"Ye Freeborn Hearts" (anon.)	584

1748

"Be Content" (anon.)	84
"The Conqur'd Strephon" (Davis)	132
"As Cloe Came into the Room" (Larken)	181
"To a Young Lady Playing on the Organ" (anon.)	228
"Monsieur Pantin" (anon.)	324
"Jove, When He Saw My Fanny's Face" (Count St. Germain)	372
"The Shepherd's Wedding" (Worgan)	420
"To Make the Wife Kind" (anon.)	468
"Hymn for Christmas Day" (Wright)	516
"Child of the Summer" (Filippo Palma)	569

1749

"L. A.'s Evening Hymn" (Stubley)	36
"The Faithful Lover" (Davies)	84
"While Pensive on the Lonely Plain" (Stubley)	275
"Ye Mortals Whom Fancies and Troubles Perplex" (anon.)	323
"The Masquerade Song" (anon.)	371
"Too Late for Redress" (anon.)	425
"Bid Me Not Love!" (Clayton)	466
"The Diffident Lover" (anon.)	518
"The Power of Beauty" (Stubley)	565

1750

"Come, Come, My Friends, Your Glasses Fill" (anon.)	84
"Don Jumpedo" (anon. dance)	132
"Push Away the Brisk Bow" (anon.)	132
"Tom Jones" (anon. dance)	179
"Contented All Day I Will Sit at Your Side" (anon.)	179
"The Complaint" (anon.)	227
"A Trip to Hanover" (anon. dance)	227
"Contentment" (anon.)	275
"The Marine Joke" (anon. dance)	276
"The Highland Laddie" (anon.)	325
"The Address to Sylvia" (Handel)	371
"Worse for Better" (anon. dance)	371
"Jocky" (anon.)	420
"When E'er for Each Other" (Allcock)	469
"Sick of the Town" (J. H———ll)	521
"Je voulois de l'amour" (anon.)	563

1751

"Tendre fruit des pleurs de l'Aurore" (A la Rose)	37
"The Sow in the Sack" (anon. dance)	37
"Pitty Patty" (Arne)	83

1754

1755

APPENDIX C
Selected Bibliography of Eighteenth-Century
Song Literature with Music, to 1760

Amaryllis. 2d ed. 2 vols. London: Lewer, 1760.

Calliope; or, English Harmony. 2 vols. London: Roberts, 1739–46.

Cantus, Songs and Fancies. Aberdeen: Forbes, 1662.

A Choice Collection of 180 Loyal Songs. 3d ed. London: N. T., 1685.

Clio and Euterpe; or, British Harmony. Vol. 1. London: Roberts, 1758.

A Collection of Original Scotch Songs. London: Walsh, [1731].

Monthly Melody; or, Polite Amusements for Gentlemen and Ladies. London: Kearsley, 1760.

The Muses Delight. Liverpool: Sadler, 1754.

The Musical Century. 2 vols. London: Carey, 1737–40.

The Musical Entertainer. 2 vols. London: Bickham [vol. 1]; Corbett [vol. 2], ca. 1737.

The Musical Miscellany. 6 vols. London: Watts, 1729–31.

Orpheus Britannicus: A Collection of All the Choicest Songs . . . by Mr. Henry Purcell. 3d ed. 2 vols. London: Playford, 1721.

Orpheus Caledonius. 2 vols. London: Thomson, 1733.

A Pocket Companion for Gentlemen and Ladies. London: Cluer, 1725.

The Scots Musical Museum. 6 vols. Edinburgh: Johnson, 1771–1803. [Although published after 1760, this collection of 600 Scottish songs is the most comprehensive eighteenth-century collection of its genre.]

A Second Set of Scots Songs. Edinburgh: Bremner, [1757].

The Songs of Scotland prior to Burns. Edited by Robert Chambers. Edinburgh: Chambers, 1862. [A particularly valuable post-1760 source for Scottish songs of the Tuesday Club era.]

Thirty Scots Songs for a Voice and Harpsichord, the Music Taken from the Most Genuine Sets Extant, the Words from Allan Ramsay. Edinburgh: Bremner, [1757].

Twelve Scots Songs for a Voice or Guitar with a Thorough Bass, Adapted for That Instrument by Robert Bremner. Edinburgh: Bremner, [1760].

Universal Harmony. London: Newbury, 1745.

Wit and Mirth; or, Pills to Purge Melancholy. 4th ed. 6 vols. London: Tonson, 1719–20.

SELECTED BIBLIOGRAPHY

Primary Sources

American Magazine, Nov. 1746.

Anne Arundel County Inventories. 1676–1776. Maryland Hall of Records, Annapolis, Md.

Anne Arundel County Inventories, Analysis of Contents. National Endowment for the Humanities, Grant No. 0067-79-0738. Compiled by Nancy Baker. Annapolis: Historic Annapolis, 1979–.

Archives of Maryland. Vol. 6. Baltimore: Maryland Historical Society, 1888.

Bacon, Thomas. "An Account of What Passed at a Meeting of the Clergy at Annapolis in October 1753, with Other Matters Relating Thereto." *Maryland Historical Magazine* 2 (1908): 364–84.

———. *A Compleat System of the Revenue of Ireland, in Its Several Branches of Import, Export, and Inland Duties*. Dublin: Reilly, 1737.

———. *Four Sermons, Preached at the Parish Church of St. Peter, in Talbot County, in the Province of Maryland . . . Viz. Two Sermons to Black Slaves, and Two Sermons for the Benefit of a Charity Working-School, in the Above Parish, for the Maintenance and Education of Orphans and Poor Children, and Negroes*. London: Oliver, 1753.

———. *Laws of Maryland at Large*. Annapolis: Green, 1765.

———. Letters. Callister Papers. Maryland Diocesan Archives, Baltimore, Md.

Bacon, Thomas, and Cecilius Calvert. *An Answer to the Queries on the Proprietary Government of Maryland, Inserted in the Public Ledger, Also an Answer to Remarks upon a Message Sent by the Lower House of Assembly of Maryland, 1762. Published in 1763, Containing a Defence of the Lord-Proprietor from the Calumnies and Misrepresentations of the Remarker; and Also a Relative to a Supply Bill for His Majesty's Service, by a Friend to Maryland*. London: n.p., 1764.

Baltimore County Inventories. Maryland Hall of Records, Annapolis, Md.

Black, William. "Journal of William Black [1744]." Edited by R. A. Brock. *Pennsylvania Magazine of History and Biography* 1 (1877): 117–32, 233–49, 404–19.

Bray, Thomas. *Bibliotheca Americanae, Quadripartitae*. London: n.p., 1709.

———. *Bibliotheca Parochialis*, pt. 1. London: E. Holt for Robert Clavel, 1697.

———. *An Essay toward Promoting All Necessary and Useful Knowledge Both Divine and Human*. London: E. Holt for Robert Clavel, 1697.

Calendar of Maryland State Papers, No. 1, The Black Books. [Abstract of ca. 1763 petition.] Annapolis: State of Maryland Publications of the Hall of Records Commission, 1943.

Calendar of State Papers, Colonial Series, America and the West Indies. May 15, 1696–
Oct. 31, 1697. London: His Majesty's Stationery Office, 1910.

Callister, Henry. Letters. Callister Papers. Maryland Diocesan Archives, Baltimore, Md.

Chancery Record. Liber P.C., 1671–1712. Maryland Hall of Records, Annapolis,
Md.

Cooke, Ebenezer. *The Sot-Weed Factor.* 1708. Reprint, edited by Bernard C.
Steiner, in *Early Maryland Poetry.* Baltimore: Murphy, 1900.

Dorsey, Caleb. Account Book. MS. 717. D. S. Ridgely Papers (1733–1884). Maryland Historical Society, Baltimore, Md.

Dublin Gazette, 1742–43.

Dublin Mercury, 1742.

Fithian, Philip Vickers. *Journal & Letters of Philip Vickers Fithian, 1773–74: A
Plantation Tutor of the Old Dominion.* Edited by Hunter Dickinson Farish.
Williamsburg, Va.: Colonial Williamsburg, 1943.

Frederick County Inventories. 1769. Box 6, folder 38. Court House, Frederick,
Maryland.

Gentleman's Magazine. London, 1744–55.

George Whitefield's Journals. London: Banner of Truth Trust, 1960.

Hamilton, Alexander. "Annapolis Md. Tuesday Club Record Book." [The minutes of each meeting, 1745–56, first version.] The Johns Hopkins University
Library, Baltimore, Md.

———. *Gentleman's Progress: The Itinerarium of Dr. Alexander Hamilton, 1744.*
Edited by Carl Bridenbaugh. Chapel Hill: University of North Carolina
Press, 1948.

———. "The History of the Ancient and Honorable Tuesday Club." 3 vols.
1754–56. The Johns Hopkins University Library, Baltimore, Md.

———. "The History of the Ancient and Honorable Tuesday Club." Vol. 3,
pp. 503–64. MS. 1265. Dulany Papers. Maryland Historical Society, Baltimore, Md.

———. *Itinerarium, Being a Narrative of a Journey from Annapolis, Maryland through
Delaware, Pennsylvania, New York, New Jersey, Connecticut, Rhode Island, Massa-
chusetts and New Hampshire from May to September, 1744.* Edited by Albert
Bushnell Hart. St. Louis: Bixby, 1907.

———. Letters. Dulany Papers. Maryland Historical Society, Baltimore, Md.

———. "Record of the Tuesday Club, Vol. I." [Second version of the minutes.]
MS. 854. Manuscripts Division, Maryland Historical Society, Baltimore, Md.

———. "Record of the Tuesday Club, Vol. II." Microfilm MS. 17137, reel no. 68,
item 170. Manuscripts Division, Peter Force Collection, Library of Congress,
Washington, D.C.

———. *Records of the Tuesday Club of Annapolis, 1745–56.* Edited by Elaine G.
Breslaw. Urbana: University of Illinois Press, 1988.

Holdsworth, Edward. *Muscipula: The Mouse-trap; or, The Battle of the Cambrians &
Mice, a Poem . . . Translated into English, by R. Lewis.* Annapolis, Md.: Parks,
1728.

Hutchinson, William. *History of the County of Cumberland.* Carlisle, Eng.: n.p.,
1794.

Jefferson, Thomas. *Notes on Virginia*. London: J. Stockdale, 1787.

London Magazine, Nov. 1745.

McMahon, John V. L. *Historical View of the Government of Maryland*. Baltimore: Lukas and Deaver, 1831.

Malcolm, Alexander. *A Treatise of Musick, Speculative, Practical, and Historical*. Edinburgh: n.p., 1721.

Maryland Gazette, 1745–59.

New York Mercury, 1753–54.

Oldmixon, John. *The British Empire in America*. London: Nicholson, Tooke, 1708.

Ormsby, John. Manuscript book of minuets inscribed "Annapolis, 1758." Library and Museum of the Performing Arts, Lincoln Center, New York.

Pennsylvania Chronicle, June 23, 1768.

Queen Anne's County Free School Minute Book. MS. 683. Manuscripts Division, Maryland Historical Society, Baltimore, Md.

Richardson, Samuel. *The History of Sir Charles Grandison*. Vol. 7. London: author, 1754.

Rubsamen, Walter, ed. *The Ballad Opera*. 28 vols. New York: Garland, 1974. [Reprints of most eighteenth-century ballad operas.]

St. Anne's Parish Register. Maryland Hall of Records, Annapolis, Md.

St. Anne's Parish Vestry Minutes. Maryland Hall of Records, Annapolis, Md.

St. Paul's Parish Records. 2 vols. Microfilm 994. Maryland Hall of Records, Annapolis, Md.

Sharpe, [Governor] Horatio. Letter to Frederick Calvert, Lord Baltimore, May 23, 1760. *Archives of Maryland*. Vol. 9. Baltimore: Maryland Historical Society, 1890.

Simpson, Christopher. *The Principles of Practicle Musick . . . Either in Singing or Playing upon an Instrument*. London: W. Godbid for Henry Brome, 1665.

Tans'ur, William. *A New Musical Grammar*. London, 1746.

Virginia Gazette, Mar. 28, 1755; June 13, 1768.

Vital Records of Marblehead, Massachusetts to the End of the Year 1849. Vol. 2. Salem, Mass.: Essex Institute, 1904.

SECONDARY SOURCES

I. BOOKS AND ARTICLES

Andrews, Charles. *The Colonial Period*. New Haven: Yale University Press, 1934.

Backus, Edythe N. *Catalogue of Music in the Huntington Library Printed before 1801*. San Marino, Calif.: Huntington Library, 1949.

Chase, Gilbert. *America's Music: From the Pilgrims to the Present*. 2d rev. ed. New York: McGraw-Hill, 1966.

Davis, Deering. *Annapolis Houses, 1700–1775*. New York: Bonanza Books, n.d.

Davis, Richard B. *Intellectual Life in the Colonial South*. 3 vols. Knoxville: University of Tennessee Press, 1978.

Epstein, Dena J. *Sinful Tunes and Spirituals: Black Folk Music to the Civil War*. Music in American Life. Urbana: University of Illinois Press, 1977.

Fiske, Roger. *English Theatre Music in the Eighteenth Century*. London: Oxford University Press, 1973.

Fuld, James J., and Mary Wallace Davidson. *18th-Century American Secular Music Manuscripts: An Inventory*. Philadelphia: Music Library Association, 1980.

Gagey, Edmond M. *Ballad Opera*. New York: Columbia University Press, 1937.

Greene, Evarts B., and Virginia D. Harrington. *American Population before the Federal Census of 1790*. 1932. Reprint. Gloucester, Mass.: Smith, 1966.

Hamm, Charles. *Music in the New World*. New York: W. W. Norton, 1983.

Harrison, Samuel A., and Oswald Tilghman. *History of Talbot County, Maryland*. 2 vols. Baltimore: William and Wilkens, 1915.

Heintze, James R. "Malcolm, Alexander." *The New Grove Dictionary of Music and Musicians*, edited by Stanley Sadie, 11:568. London: Macmillan, 1980.

Hemphill, John. "Annapolis: Colonial Metropolis and State Capital." In *The Old Line State*, edited by Morris L. Radoff. Baltimore: Historical Record Assoc., 1956.

Holland, Eugenia Calvert, et al. *Four Generations of Commissions: The Peale Collection of the Maryland Historical Society*. Baltimore: Maryland Historical Society, 1975.

Hughes-Hughes, Augustus. *Catalogue of Manuscript Music in the British Museum*. 3 vols. 1906–9. Reprint. London: Trustees of the British Museum, 1964–66.

Jacobsen, Phebe R. *Quaker Records in Maryland*. Annapolis, Md.: Hall of Records Commission, 1966.

Keeler, G. A. "Banjo." In *Grove's Dictionary of Music and Musicians*, 5th ed., edited by Eric Blom, 1:401–3. London: Macmillan, 1954.

Keller, Kate Van Winkle. *Popular Secular Music in America through 1800: A Preliminary Checklist of Manuscripts in North American Collections*. MLA Index and Bibliography Series, no. 21. Philadelphia: Music Library Association, 1981.

Land, Aubrey C. *Colonial Maryland*. Millwood, N.Y.: Krause-Thomas, 1981.

———. "The Colonial Period." In *The Old Line State*, edited by Morris L. Radoff. Baltimore: Historical Record Assoc., 1956.

Laugher, Charles T. *Thomas Bray's Grand Design*. Chicago: American Library Assoc., 1973.

Lemay, J. A. Leo. *Men of Letters in Colonial Maryland*. Knoxville: University of Tennessee Press, 1972.

Lowens, Irving. *A Bibliography of Songsters Printed in America before 1821*. Worcester, Mass.: American Antiquarian Society, 1976.

Molnar, John W. *Songs from the Williamsburg Theatre*. Williamsburg, Va.: Colonial Williamsburg Foundation, 1972.

Owings, Donnell M. *His Lordship's Patronage*. Baltimore: Maryland Historical Society, 1953.

Papenfuse, Edward. *In Pursuit of Profit*. Baltimore: The Johns Hopkins University Press, 1975.

Papenfuse, Edward, Alan F. Day, David W. Jordan, and Gregory A. Stiverson. *A Biographical Dictionary of the Maryland Legislature, 1635–1789*. 2 vols. Baltimore: The Johns Hopkins University Press, 1979.

Rabson, Carolyn, and Kate Van Winkle Keller. *The National Tune Index*. New York: University Music Editions, 1980.

Rankin, Hugh F. *The Theater in Colonial America*. Chapel Hill: University of North Carolina Press, 1965.

Reps, John. *Tidewater Towns*. Williamsburg, Va.: Colonial Williamsburg Foundation, 1972.

Schnapper, Edith B., ed. *The British Union-Catalogue of Early Music Printed before the Year 1801*. London: Buttersworth, 1957.

Schultz, Edward T. *History of Freemasonry in Maryland*. 3 vols. Baltimore: Medairy, 1884.

Seilhamer, George O. *History of the American Theatre*. Philadelphia: Globe Printing House, 1888.

Simpson, Claude M. *The British Broadside Ballad and Its Music*. New Brunswick: Rutgers University Press, 1966.

Sonneck, Oscar G. T. *Early Concert-Life in America (1731–1800)*. 1907. Reprint. New York: Da Capo Press, 1978.

———. *Francis Hopkinson: The First American Poet-Composer (1737–1791), and James Lyon: Patriot, Preacher, Psalmodist (1735–1794)*. 1905. Reprint, with a new introduction by Richard Crawford. New York: Da Capo Press, 1966.

Squire, William Barclay. *Catalogue of Printed Music Published between 1487 and 1800 Now in the British Museum*. 1912. Reprint. Nendeln, Liechtenstein: Kraus, 1968.

Ulrich, Homer. *Chamber Music*. New York: Columbia University Press, 1948.

Van Cleef, Joy, and Kate Van Winkle Keller. "Selected American Country Dances and Their English Sources." In *Music in Colonial Massachusetts, 1630–1820*. Vol. 1, *Music in Public Places*, Publications of the Colonial Society of Massachusetts, vol. 53. Boston: Colonial Society of Massachusetts, 1980.

Wertenbaker, Thomas J. *The Golden Age of Colonial Culture*. New York: New York University Press, 1942.

Whitehill, Walter Muir. *Independent Historical Societies*. Boston: Boston Athenaeum, 1962.

Wilson, Everett B. *American Colonial Mansions and Other Early Houses*. New York: Barnes, 1965.

Wright, Louis B. *The Cultural Life of the American Colonies, 1607–1763*. New York: Harper and Row, 1957.

Wroth, Lawrence C. *A History of Printing in Colonial Maryland*. Baltimore: Typothetae, 1922.

II. DISSERTATIONS, THESES, AND PAPERS

Breslaw, Elaine G. "Dr. Alexander Hamilton and the Enlightenment in Maryland." Ph.D. diss., University of Maryland, 1973.

Heintze, James R. "Music in Colonial Annapolis." M.A. thesis, American University, 1969.

Micklus, Robert J. "Dr. Alexander Hamilton's 'The History of the Tuesday Club.'" 4 vols. Ph.D. diss., University of Delaware, 1980.

Moss, Harold Gene. "Ballad-Opera Songs: A Record of Ideas Set to Music, 1728–1733." 4 vols. Ph.D. diss., University of Michigan, 1970.

Stone, Reppard. "An Evaluative Study of Alexander Malcolm's 'Treatise of Music: Speculative, Practical and Historical.'" Ph.D. diss., Catholic University, 1974.

Talley, John B. "The Tuesday Club Manuscripts: Annapolis, 1745–1756." Paper presented at the annual conference of the Sonneck Society, Baltimore, Mar. 23, 1980.

III. PERIODICALS

Allen, Ethan. "Rev. Thomas Bacon." *American Quarterly Church Review* 17 (Oct. 1865): 430–51.

Breslaw, Elaine G. "The Chronicle as Satire: Dr. Alexander Hamilton's History of the Tuesday Club." *Maryland Historical Magazine* 70 (1975): 129–48.

———. "An Early Maryland Musical Society." *Maryland Historical Magazine* 67 (1972): 436–37.

———. "Wit, Whimsy, and Politics: The Uses of Satire by the Tuesday Club of Annapolis, 1744[5]–1756." *William and Mary Quarterly*, 3d ser., 32 (1975): 295–306.

Deibert, William E. "Thomas Bacon, Colonial Clergyman." *Maryland Historical Magazine* 73 (1978): 79–86.

Fletcher, Charlotte. "The Reverend Thomas Bray, M. Alexander Vattemare, and Library Science." *Library Quarterly* 27 (1957): 95–99.

Flood, W. H. Grattan. "Eighteenth Century Italians in Dublin." *Music & Letters* 3 (1922): 274–78.

Freeman, Sarah E. "The Tuesday Club Medal." *Numismatist* 57 (1945): 1313–22.

Heintze, James R. "Alexander Malcolm, Musician, Clergyman, and Schoolmaster." *Maryland Historical Magazine* 73 (1978): 226–35.

Karinen, Arthur E. "Maryland Population." *Maryland Historical Magazine* 54 (1959): 365–407.

———. "Numerical and Distributional Aspects of Maryland Population, 1631–1840." *Maryland Historical Magazine* 60 (1965): 139–59.

Maurer, Maurer. "Alexander Malcolm in America." *Music & Letters* 33 (1952): 226.

———. "The Library of a Colonial Musician, 1755." *William and Mary Quarterly*, 3d ser., 7 (1950): 39–52.

Molnar, John W. "A Collection of Music in Colonial Virginia: The Ogle Inventory." *Musical Quarterly* 49 (1963): 150–62.

Steiner, Bernard Christian. "The Reverend Thomas Bray and His American Libraries." *American Historical Review* 2 (1896): 59–75.

Tyler, John W. "Foster Cunliffe and Sons: Liverpool Merchants in the Maryland Tobacco Trade, 1738–1765." *Maryland Historical Magazine* 73 (1978): 246–79.

Ward, Kathryn P. "The First Professional Theater in Maryland in Its Colonial Setting." *Maryland Historical Magazine* 70 (1975): 29–44.

Weekly, Carolyn J. "Portrait Painting in Eighteenth-Century Annapolis." *Magazine Antiques*, Feb. 1977, pp. 345–53.

Wheeler, Joseph Towne. "Booksellers and Circulating Libraries in Colonial Maryland." *Maryland Historical Magazine* 34 (1939): 111–37.

———. "Books Owned by Marylanders, 1700–1776." *Maryland Historical Magazine* 35 (1940): 337–53.

———. "The Laymen's Libraries and the Provincial Library." *Maryland Historical Magazine* 35 (1940): 60–73.

———. "Literary Culture in Eighteenth Century Maryland, 1700–1776." *Maryland Historical Magazine* 38 (1943): 273–76.

———. "Reading and Other Recreations of Marylanders, 1700–1776." *Maryland Historical Magazine* 38 (1943): 37–55, 167–80.

———. "Reading Interests of Maryland Planters and Merchants, 1700–1776." *Maryland Historical Magazine* 37 (1942): 26–41, 291–310.

———. "Reading Interests of the Professional Classes in Colonial Maryland, 1700–1776." *Maryland Historical Magazine* 36 (1941): 184–201, 281–301.

———. "Thomas Bray and the Maryland Parochial Libraries." *Maryland Historical Magazine* 34 (1939): 246–55.

Wroth, Lawrence C. "A Maryland Merchant and His Friends in 1750." *Maryland Historical Magazine* 6 (1911): 213–40.

PART II
MUSIC

Figure 3. Facsimile of title page to the Anniversary Ode
of 1750. In Alexander Hamilton, "Record of the Tuesday Club,
Vol. I," MS. 854, Appendix, Manuscript Division, Maryland
Historical Society, Baltimore.

INTRODUCTION

The anniversary odes and incidental instrumental music composed by members of the Tuesday Club are found in the two principal club documents; Alexander Hamilton's "Record of the Tuesday Club, Vol. I," MS. 854, Manuscripts Division, Maryland Historical Society, Baltimore, and in his "History of the Ancient and Honorable Tuesday Club," 3 vols. (1754–56), in both The Johns Hopkins University Library, Baltimore, and Maryland Historical Society. Much of the music appears in both sources, except for the following pieces found only in the "History": the vocal setting of the 1750 ode, the "Grand Club Minuet with Variations," the entire 1753 ode, the "Minuet for the Poet Laureat," the "Grand Club Jig," and the "Overture for His Honor's Entertainment."

Both manuscript sources are in poor condition (see fig. 3). The ink has bled through the torn and crumbling pages, riddled with holes. In reconstructing the music I have preferred the "History" manuscripts (indicated in the music as "HTC"). "MS. 854" denotes the "Record" as the original source. Where neither source is indicated, the "History" is to be assumed. The abbreviation *conj.* (conjecture) identifies passages that I composed relying on standard principles of eighteenth-century counterpoint as applied by the Tuesday Club composers. My reconstructions are based on extant melodic and rhythmic patterns that recur very predictably in the binary dance forms preferred by these Annapolis composers.

The text underlay is very ambiguous in the original sources. No conventions of barring or use of slurs were used to indicate precise placement of syllables, and the alignment of words and music is often confusing. Consequently, the slur marks that indicate melismatic groupings are my own. They are based on eighteenth-century practice and have been refined in numerous public performances. Additional editorial suggestions, intended to remedy obvious copying errors or to avoid unlikely dissonances, are enclosed in brackets. Although this work is intended to be a performing edition, I have not attempted to improve compositional deficiencies in the music. Thus, there remain many instances of awkward voice leading, parallel fifths and octaves, unusual successions of harmonies, and other musical manifestations more typical of beginning students of eighteenth-century counterpoint. This compositional naïveté is an integral part of the Tuesday Club music; too many improvements would no longer accurately represent the state of music as experienced by the Annapolis amateurs.

After a number of public performances of this music, I offer these suggestions. The vocal part is very demanding. Its tessitura is high, so high that most of the songs can be sung in either the tenor range (one octave below the notated pitch) or in the bass range (two octaves lower than written), enabling all singers to join in on the choruses in a comfortable voice range. The tenor range is the most likely choice for the arias. Although high, this range is frequently encountered in contemporary songsters, and eighteenth-century pitch, while not standardized, was sometimes more than a semitone lower than the present-day A=440. Performers would be well advised to consider transposing both the songs of Part I and the odes of Part II to a more accessible range. The second violin should not double the vocal line, playing only the instrumental interludes. The original manuscripts are inconsistent in the use of repeat signs. In these sectional forms, especially the instrumental dances, all clearly defined sections should be repeated, while varying the ornamentation and dynamic levels. Not all of this music is suitable for public performance. Bacon's compositions are all quite good, and the "Gavotta Grande" in the 1753 overture as well as Thornton's jig are worth hearing. Some of Hamilton's vocal settings in the 1750 ode and a few parts of the 1753 ode are presentable, but much of these last two compositions is primarily of academic interest.

For public performance I recommend a lecture-recital format: programs chosen carefully from the original club compositions, combining these and a few of the popular songs from chapter 5 with readings from Hamilton's entertaining descriptions of performers and musical events have proven to be enjoyable and enlightening.

Music of the
ANNIVERSARY ODE
of the Tuesday Club
for the year 1750

① g♯″in HTC.

② ♯ indistinct in MS.854; absent in HTC.

③ ![music] is better; both manuscripts agree, however.

Air for his honor

allegro

Minuet for his honor

vivace

Basso Tacet ⑤

④ Repeat signs appear on both sides of double bar in HTC, second system.

⑤ MS. 854 has bass part doubling second violin; probably intended as an alternate version.
After the first measure this part is displaced by one bar – undoubtedly a copying error
since on the following page, the bass and second violin parts are correctly aligned.

⑥ These letters appear in HTC; they represent letter names as if passage were notated in G clef.

Recitativo

Ode music by Signor Secretario [7]

(1.) Thrice hail se -
(2.) Phoe - bus has

rene re - turn - ing day,   bright   day,   out - shin - ing   far   the
now five courses run,   the   lau - - reat twice   es - say'd   to

[7] *The remainder of this ode was composed by Alexander Hamilton.*

rest on which The Tues-day Club —— in May first
Sing great Jole's —— e - clat, that glo-rious man, from

rear'd her gay & So - cial Crest.
whence the Club's best bless-ings Spring.

Aria Symphonio Con Spirito

⑧ g and e are on separate pages; the g is apparently tied to the first note of the following
 page which is an e ; therefore, e was probably correct.

④ Suggest B ; e is clear in manuscript.
⑩ Invertible counterpoint; see m. 87.

Sound-ing, Soft-er ech-o-ing flutes re - bound - ing, Cel - e -brate a day so

bright, Cel - e -brate a __ day so bright. Shouts of tri - umph, peals of

Joy, Shouts of tri - umph, peals of Joy, ————— in praise of

our de-light, A-pol - lo height-ens our____ de - light.

Chorus

For-tune ev-er chang-ing, now Shall___ keep from Rang-ing &

with great Jole Shall live, & with great Jole Shall live.

⑪ Typical: either the first or second treble functions reasonably well with the bass; the three parts sounded together produce unlikely dissonances.

⑫ The entire passage (mm. 112–14) can also be played as triplets.

    — & with great Jole Shall live, — and with great Jole — Shall live.

⑬ Probably should imitate m. 123: octave leaps.

Recitativo

Hon-or & Jus-tice on each side the Chair, be-hold, while Jole, Sits there in State, Se-
-cure. Our knight, with cour-age rare— and front ter-ri-fic, guards the aw-ful Seat.

Symphonia furioso

Should an-y bold in-trud-er dare _____

to as-sault the

Club　　　or Storm the Chair_____

⑭ Measures 160-67 of the first violin part are displaced by one bar in HTC; a copying error.

Chair, or Storm the Chair, his bones Sir John would

fall up-on, and fu-rious-ly at

ev-ery bang, de-mand a

15 e' or 𝄽; the f#' fits with the third beat of m. 161, where it appears in the original manuscript (see preceding note).

prompt e - clair - cis - se - ment, a prompt e - clair - cisse - ment.

⑯ Chorus

Till bruis'd to mash, & crushed to pow-der   a _____ pit- - - eous

⑯ The first six measures may be successfully performed in the key of G, with only one sharp shifting to two sharps in m. 193.

⑰ There are five beats in this bar.

⑱ Manuscript very faint: for m. 198, reconstructed to match similar phrase in mm. 199-200; same text. This passage may be played using only one sharp until m. 202.

⑲ Measures 201-5 show many alterations and added notes; evidently an attempt was made to improve this passage.

⑳ There are five beats in this bar; alignment suggests that the d was added; recommend delete e.

he flies_elsewhere to re-con - noi-tre, to re-con-

noi - - - - - - - tre, to re-con-noi-tre, to re-con-noi-tre.

Recitativo

[1.] High in the Chair with look profound Il -
[2.] He with a Sage Important face, most

- lustrious Jole dis-pens-es round, aw-ful but Just au-thor-i-ty.
graceful fills his lof-ty place, promoting mirth & Jol - li-ty.

㉑ The bass passage in mm. 204-5 has been so altered that it is illegible;
probable final version appears above the treble in the original manuscript.

Aria Symphonica affettuosa

A- pol - lo with his band ___ of ___ Singers the tune - - - ful nine ___ the ___ Chair ___ Sur - round, he

22 see m. 224
23 see m. 215
24 Copyist has simply repeated bass line, mm. 219-20; probable copying error; suggest transposing entire passage, mm. 225-28

See, to all our members Long & Standing are bounteous too, as well as She, and all their choicest gifts are send-ing.

Aria, Symphonia Con Spirito

㉕ Change of key signature probably a copying error; C♯s are still notated as accidentals (mm. 283, 288–90).

bound, and bowls go round, Let mirth a - bound, and bowls go round. _____

_____ Let mirth a - bound, a - bound _____ and bowls go round, go round

to _____ hon - or _____ Jole, _____ our life & Soul, to hon - or

㉖ Transpose a third lower.

Jole _____ our ___ life _____ our life and Soul.

Symphonia

pianissimo

forte

㉗ Compare mm. 316-24 and 270-78 for melodic variation; the e' in m. 270 is probably an error and should correspond to m. 272; however, the da capo (m. 316) is the same in this regard.

each sad thought be cleared _____ a - way.

Grand Chorus

While Jole shall live ___ to fill ___ our chair,

we ___ ev - er ___ Shall ___ be ___ deb - o - nair,

㉘ Violin I should match violin II ; compare mm. 348 and 367.

kind heaven ___ grant ___ that long ___ he ___ may re-

main ___ in health to bless this day, re-

main [in health] in health ___ to ___ bless ___ this day, re-

main [in health,] in __ health, ____ re - main in health to __ bless   this

day,   long   live,   long   live   the   Tues - day

Club,   long   live ,   long   live   the   Tues-day

Music of the Anniversary ode
for the year 1751

by Signior Lardini [Thomas Bacon]

① "Jole" in HTC; "Cole" in MS.854. "Cole" is the earlier form of the president's name.

Aria con spirito

bright from that— ex- al -ted Chair, up -on — this an -cient Club. May

no ill na-tured gout -y pain May no ill na- tured gout -y pain,

e'er— in -vade those limbs a - gain— us of— our Joy— to rob.

Ye Muses nine, at-tend my call, Cole's praise to Sing, I need you all Had I [Had I] a hundred tongues, a hundred tongues and lungs of brass, My bra-zen lungs and hundred tongues, this mighty, mighty theme would far sur-pass.

ous   Sir   Hugh   Sub - mits__to__his__su - per - ior   mer - it

Club March against Sir Hugh Maccarty

a Tempo Giusto

[MS. 854: Grand Chorus which ought to be accompanied w Trumpets, Kettle Drums, &tc.]

Long live Il - lus - trious Cole,   Long live Il - lus - trious

Cole   Long live Il - lus - trious Cole,   the Chair to

him we stand and fall   he   is   our   glo - ry   he   is our

Glo - ry   he   is our   glo - ry our joy, our   all.

he   is   our   Glo - ry   he   is our   Glo - ry

Variatione [I]

Minuet for Sir John

[Thomas Bacon]

conspirito

Minuet for his honor ~ by Sign.r Lardini

[Thomas Bacon]

MUSIC of the ANNIVERSARY ODE
for the year 1753 *

By Several hands

* Much of this ode can be improved by reducing the number of parts from three to two, thereby eliminating octave and unison doubling, as well as extraneous third-voice passages.

Minuet for the Chancellor

① Stems appear in original manuscript, but note heads are cut off.
② Accidental is unclear in manuscript – probably ♮
③ Sharp in manuscript is probably an error. The bass line is missing for most of mm. 37-40; conjecture derived from similar passages in mm. 29, 59-60.

Violincello Solo

④ Measures 88-92 are illegible. Also possible : DC al fine at m.75.

Symphonia Solo

Sing__ a - gain with might __ &

main the Club and glo - rious Jole, Sing a-
[f]

[omit the g"s - - -]

gain with might — & main, the Club — & glo-ri-ous

Jole, the Club — & glo - - rious Jole.

[3] [ᴧᴧ]   [ᴧᴧ]

⑤ This measure is missing in the original manuscript – refer to opening of the Symphonia Solo, m. 93.

ⓖ Original manuscript displaced by one bar, mm. 235-39

o'er the wide   wel - kin Jole's   fame loud - ly flies,   and

o'er the wide   wel - kin, Jole's   fame loud - ly   flies.

Minuet for his honor

Gavotte for his honor

allegro

⑦ Upper parts should remain in octaves on third beat, mm. 286 and 287.

Recitativo

In grand Consisto- ry, the members met, Jole at their head, in

throne ma-jes-tic set. Say Bard, who e'er a nob-ler Jun-to saw,

who rules   like   Jole, or who like Jole __ gives __ Law,   all   ot - her

pres- i-dents to him   are   Scrubs,   & his   is Sure the   par - a - gon   of Clubs.

Whilst the   val-iant Sir John, __ Sits close by his Chair o, Sits   Close by his Chair o, Sits

Close by his Chair o', his   hon - or fears none, __ nor   here o, nor there o, nor

here o nor there o ,nor here o nor there o.

Fol de ral de, lol de ral de

[lol de ral de lol de ral] For his Shining Sword, the

best blade in   nature, the best blade in na-ture, the   best blade in na-ture lops

off like a gourd, the head of each traitor, the head of   each traitor, the

head of each traitor

Minuet for Sir John

March for Sir John

⑧ Probably octaves with bass

⑨ Suggest omitting the second violin part from here through m. 409.

General Grand Chorus

Then all with one voice ___ & turned ___ up eyes ___

lets Sing & re - joice, praising Jole to the Skies

O Jole, migh-ty Jole, 'tis

thee we pro - claim with voice, drum & trum-pet we'll

sound forth thy   name   of Rul-ers the   Chief   &   presidents

to ___ our   Joy & re - lief, ___ comes   on-ly from   you, then a-

way with all   grief, we'll be   mer - ry &   true.   Then Huzza for Great

⑩ Not a copying error; see similar cadences in mm. 471 and 479.

Jole & Huzza for great Jole, our bless-ing light on his mag-

na-ni-mous Soul, with plea-sure we'll dub him head of our

Club & top off his health in a full flow-ing bowl, with

⑪ Original displaced by one bar.

pleasure we'll dub ___ him head of our Club ___ &

top off his health ___ in full flow - ing bowl.

Minuet for the Poet Laureat

⑫ Original was notated a second higher, mm. 15-24.

⑬ Original was notated a third higher, mm. 25-27.

Grand Club Jig by Signor Proto musicus   [William Thornton]

violini unisoni

⑭ Original displaced by one bar.

Overture for his honor's Entertainment, by Signor Lardini
[Overture for the 1752 Anniversary Ode by Thomas Bacon]

Gavotta Burlesqua for his honor by Sign.r Lardini

Minuet for the Attorney General by Sign[r] Lardini   [Thomas Bacon]

Ex Libris
Johannis Ormsby

Annapolis

January the 30th 1758

A Minuet in Signor Martini's Sonatas

Widiman's Minuet

A Minuet by the Rever.ᵈ Mr. Bacon

Geminiani's Minuet

A Minuet in Sampson by M.ʳ Handel

A minuet by Corelli

The Dutchess of Areaster's Minuet

New Bath Minuet

Auretta's Minuet

Philadelphia Minuet

Minuet by Signior Martini

Lord Holderness Minuet

Gardini's Minuet

Mis Hopkisson's Minuet

Dubourg's Minuet

A Favorite Minuet

Signior Martini's Favorite Minuet

The King of Prussia's Minuet

A Minuet

A Minuet by Signior Lacatelli

A Minuet

A Minuet

Minuet by Mr Humphries

Minuet by Mr Barrish

INDEX

A Note on the Author

A native of Princeton, Kentucky, John Barry Talley earned a bachelor of music degree from the Oberlin College Conservatory of Music, Oberlin, Ohio, and received his master's and doctorate in music from the Peabody Institute of The Johns Hopkins University in Baltimore. In addition to his wide-ranging experience as a performer, he has done extensive research on eighteenth-century British secular music. He is currently director of musical activities at the United States Naval Academy.

N.B. For further information on the Tuesday Club, see Elaine G. Breslaw, ed., *Records of the Tuesday Club of Annapolis, 1745–56*, the companion volume to the present work.

Resources of American Music History: A Directory of Source
Materials from Colonial Times to World War II
D. W. KRUMMEL, JEAN GEIL, DORIS J. DYEN, AND DEANE L. ROOT

Tenement Songs: The Popular Music of the Jewish Immigrants
MARK SLOBIN

Ozark Folksongs
VANCE RANDOLPH
EDITED AND ABRIDGED BY NORM COHEN

Oscar Sonneck and American Music
EDITED BY WILLIAM LICHTENWANGER

Bluegrass Breakdown: The Making of the Old Southern Sound
ROBERT CANTWELL

Bluegrass: A History
NEIL V. ROSENBERG

Music at the White House: A History of the American Spirit
ELISE K. KIRK

Red River Blues: The Blues Tradition in the Southeast
BRUCE BASTIN

Good Friends and Bad Enemies: Robert Winslow Gordon
and the Study of American Folksong
DEBORA KODISH

Fiddlin' Georgia Crazy: Fiddlin' John Carson, His Real World,
and the World of His Songs
GENE WIGGINS

America's Music: From the Pilgrims to the Present,
Revised Third Edition
GILBERT CHASE

Secular Music in Colonial Annapolis: The Tuesday Club, 1745-56
JOHN BARRY TALLEY